D0607241

FATHERHOOD

and other stories

Thomas H. Cook

PEGASUS CRIME
NEW YORK LONDON

FATHERHOOD

Pegasus Books LLC
80 Broad Street, 5th Floor
New York, NY 10004

Copyright © 2013 by Thomas H. Cook

First Pegasus Books edition 2013

Interior design by Maria Fernandez

All rights reserved. No part of this book may be reproduced in whole or in part
without written permission from the publisher, except by reviewers who may quote
brief excerpts in connection with a review in a newspaper, magazine, or electronic
publication; nor may any part of this book be reproduced, stored in a retrieval system,
or transmitted in any form or by any means electronic, mechanical, photocopying,
recording, or other, without written permission from the publisher.

Library of Congress Cataloging-in-Publication Data is available.

ISBN: 978-1-60598-467-4

10 9 8 7 6 5 4 3 2 1

Printed in the United States of America
Distributed by W. W. Norton & Company

To Claiborne Hancock

for collecting a lifetime of short stories into this single volume.

CONTENTS

CONVICTION

The phone rang at six in the morning.

J. R. Ballard grabbed the receiver, squeezed it like a chicken neck.

"Ballard here."

He'd thought that maybe, just maybe, it being the morning after Confederate Memorial Day, the bigwigs downtown might have considered a slow start. But that illusion died on the back of Eddie McCorkindale's boyishly excited voice.

"Got something Chief Langford wants you to see, J.R."

He meant Newport Langford, Chief of Detectives, Atlanta Police, a polite, well-mannered man, almost courtly, who had, over the years, come to trust Ballard more than anyone else in Homicide.

"And what might that be?" Ballard asked.

"A girl."

Ballard languidly stroked his substantial jowls. "A girl not altogether well, I take it?"

"Dead," McCorkindale said. "White. Thirteen—fourteen. Something like that."

"What happened to her?"

"Beat up, looks like. Strangled, too. Been dead about twelve hours or so, we guess."

The "we," as J.R. surmised, was probably McCorkindale and a few other layabouts who, despite their rank stupidity, held to the dream, more of a fantasy, that they might one day be competent homicide detectives. The guess was precisely that, with nothing to back it up but the thoroughly unjustified self-confidence of those who'd made it.

"In a basement," McCorkindale added. "On Forsyth Street."

"Whereabouts?"

"Over next to the coal chute."

"I don't mean whereabouts in the basement, Eddie," Ballard said crisply, though not without trying to keep the tone of condescension from his voice. "I mean whereabouts on Forsyth Street."

"Oh. National Pencil Company. You know it?"

Of course he knew it, but J.R. let it go.

"We're trying to locate the guy who runs the place."

"I wouldn't even bother with that, Eddie," J.R. said.

"You wouldn't? How come?"

"Because there is a likely suspect," J.R. said. "A colored man who works at the building. He's been in a good deal of trouble before now."

"Colored man? Would that be Newt Lee?"

"No, that would not be Newt Lee," J.R. said, no longer able to keep the snappishness from his voice. "Newt Lee is a family man. A fine man, by all accounts. I'm talking about the roustabout. Jim Conley." He drew in a soft, weary breath. "Follow me here, Eddie. You have a dead girl in the pencil factory, and you have a colored man of very low reputation like Conley working there. Does the logic strike you?"

"Well, the thing is, nobody's seen another one. Just Newt."

"Well, you ask Newt where Conley is, and then you go get him," J.R. said in a measured, though still not impolite tone.

"Yeah, but what . . ."

"Eddie, please," Ballard said. "Just do it."

"Okay," Eddie said. "The name's Conley, you say?"

J.R. knew he was writing it down, misspelling it, trying again, *Conly, Conlee, Konley.*

"That's right," J.R. said softly. "Jim Conley. C-O-N-L-E-Y."

"Got it, J.R."

"Good," J.R. said. He dropped the receiver back into its cradle, the murder already playing out in his mind, Conley stumbling backward, dragging a girl along the floor, out of breath and sweaty by the time he reaches the coal chute, reaching for his battered thermos, munching a banana sandwich. Case closed, J.R. thought.

———◇———

Confederate Memorial Day had been a cold, drizzling affair, and as he drove down Peachtree Street, J.R. surveyed its sodden aftermath. Drenched battle flags hung limply, dripping water from their tips. Blue and gray bunting whipped about the streets or hung in ragged clumps from trees and bushes. Some of it slumped, wet and soggy, from over doors and fence railings. It gave the whole city a miserable, defeated look, just the opposite of its original intent. The only Lost Cause it brought to J.R.'s mind was the one of finally cleaning it all up.

The National Pencil Company had once been the Granite Hotel, complete with its own theater, the Venable, and J.R. knew that its conversion into a clanging, dusty factory had irritated more than a few of Atlanta's old guard, another symbol of the "Yankeefication" of their city. But most of that sort of talk had died away over the years, replaced by the sort of sentiment J.R. saw on a large red and white poster as he wheeled onto Five Points, "Watch Atlanta Grow."

The National Pencil Factory was part of that growth, and J.R. was perfectly happy with it. He'd been born into a family of hardscrabble tenant farmers in South Georgia, lost his father in the Battle of Lookout Mountain, and had no love for the moonlight and magnolia crowd who ran Atlanta, always "stirring up the ashes," as he'd once put it, of a world their own arrogance had burned down. Thus freed from a poor boy's idolatry for his "betters," he'd struggled to acquire a certain refinement in dress and comportment, adopted an arch manner of speech he'd associated with the highly educated, and even secretly come to admire the sophisticated Northerners his rude associates in the Police Department still insisted upon calling carpetbaggers.

Luke Rogers was standing in front of the factory as J.R. pulled up.

"Good morning, J.R." he said.

"Not particularly good for one of our female citizens, I hear," J.R. said. "Have you established her identity yet?"

Rogers plucked the cigarette from the corner of his mouth. "Phagan. Mary Phagan. Worked here at the factory. Mama said she came down yesterday morning to get her pay."

J.R. lumbered toward the door, overweight to the point of being embarrassed by it. To her dying day, his mother had always described him as pleasantly plump, a lie that had signaled a world of liars in J.R.'s mind. After that, police work could not have come more naturally to him.

"Did the mother have any other pertinent information?" he asked.

"Nope."

"And the father?"

"He's a lint head."

"His occupation is irrelevant," J.R. said. "Was he of help regarding the murder?"

Rogers shook his head, opened the door as J.R. strode toward it. "The Great J. R. Ballard is now on the scene," he announced with a broad grin.

A wall of men in rumpled suits blocked J.R.'s view of the body. John Black and S.J. Starnes, both detectives, along with Craig Britt, a whiskey-soaked police reporter for the Atlanta *Constitution* whose own activities, J.R. thought, were only a notch above the criminals he covered.

As J.R. approached, the wall broke up, and he saw the girl lying on a slag heap, the left profile of her face scratched and torn, dotted here and there with splinters, smudged with coal dust.

Dragged across the floor, J.R. surmised, killed somewhere else.

The other men grumbled greetings as J.R. joined their circle, looking more closely now, carefully observing the white throat, a cord knotted around it, along with a piece of cloth, as J.R. noted immediately, torn from her petticoat. He glanced about the room, surveyed the factory's dark innards, boilers, furnaces, a coal chute, boxes of pencils scattered throughout, some open, spilling out their contents, some tied with—yes, J.R. thought—the same cord that had been used to strangle Mary Phagan.

"So, what do you think, J.R.?" Starnes asked. "Think it's the same one?"

Starnes was referring to the fact that over the last few months thirteen colored women had been murdered in Atlanta.

"Think he's jumped from the quarters to the house?"

Meaning, as J.R. knew, from black to white.

He returned his eyes to the dead girl, the few parts of her that were visible among the lavender heap of her dress and the soiled swirl of her petticoat. Her tongue protruded from her mouth. One eye was black, swollen. The real wound was at the back of her head, her scalp split open, blood in a dark, sticky wash down her back. The cord around her throat had been wrung so tightly it had bitten into her flesh, leaving a raw, red circle around her neck.

Jim Conley swam into J.R.'s mind, pop-eyed and vicious, a liar and a thief. "Could be," he said.

Rogers laughed. "Newt was shaking like a leaf when we got here," he said. "I had to practically hold him up on the way to the basement."

"Newt had nothing to do with this," J.R. said assuredly.

"What do you make of these, then?" Rogers asked. "Craig found them beside the girl." He handed J.R. two scraps of paper, one white, one brown, then shined his flashlight on them, revealing a crude scrawl. The first read "he said he wood love me and land down play like night witch did it but that long tall black negro did buy his self."

"What do you think?" Britt asked, pencil at the ready, looking for a quote.

J.R. didn't answer, went on to the second: "mam, that negro hire doun here did this I went to make water and he push me doun that hole a long tall negro black that hoo it was long sleam tall negro I wright while play with me."

"I don't have to tell you, J.R.," Rogers said. "Newt's one tall, skinny nigger."

"Here's the night watchman, too," Craig said. "Get it? In the note, I mean. Night witch. Night watch."

J.R. handed the notes back to Rogers. "Newt Lee has nothing to do with this."

Starnes nodded. "J.R.'s right. Newt wouldn't have the balls for something like this."

Britt grinned. "How 'bout the inclination? If that's strong enough, a man can grow the balls."

J.R.'s eyes slid over to Britt, then back to the girl. "Have you located Jim Conley yet?" he asked no one in particular.

"McCorkindale told us what you said about him," Starnes answered. "We're out looking for him."

"Try the rail yard," J.R. said. "Bus depot. He's probably long gone by now, but try them."

"You really think he did it, do you, J.R.?" Starnes asked.

J.R. looked at him directly. "I'm dead sure of it," he said.

Suddenly Eddie McCorkindale burst through the circle. "They found the factory manager."

Starnes laughed. "Why, was he lost?"

"Well, let's go get him," Rogers said.

J.R. didn't move.

"You don't want to come along, J.R.?" Rogers asked him.

J.R. waved his hand dismissively, then returned his gaze to the dead girl.

"Name's Frank, the factory manager," Rogers said, glancing at his notes as he and the other men headed for the door. "Leo Frank."

———◦———

J.R. was having a cigar, sitting massive behind his small wooden desk in the detective bull pen when Rogers and the others appeared again, Leo Frank in tow but barely visible as they bustled him among the empty desks toward Newport Langford's office. Watching, J.R. saw only an oily flash of black hair, a glint of spectacles, the gold wink of a cuff link, the rest obscured by a flowing curtain of wrinkled suits.

He blew a column of smoke into the air, leaned back, sniffed, planned his method of approach when they finally dragged Jim Conley into the bull pen. He was still lining up the questions, planning how he'd lurch forward from time to time, plant his huge face directly in front of Conley's, close enough, as he imagined it, for a little spit to hit him in the eye with each question, when the door to Langford's office swung open. It was a crude persona he'd adopted before, in such cases, often to hilarious, but always telling, effect.

"J.R.," Rogers called. "Chief Langford wants you in on this."

J.R. rose ponderously, put his enormous frame in motion, fat like congealed air around him, forever walking, as it seemed to him, through a thick, invisible gelatin.

The room was hot, crowded, rancid with tobacco smoke. Frank sat in a plain wooden chair, facing Newport Langford. He was dressed in a black suit, freshly starched white shirt, with gold cuff links, a small, skinny man, so short his feet dangled a good half inch above the floor. He didn't smoke, and from time to time he lifted his hand and waved away the curls of smoke that swirled around his nose and eyes. The lenses of his glasses occasionally glinted in the light that fell over him from the high window behind Langford's desk. He cleared his throat every few minutes and sometimes coughed softly into a tiny, loosely clenched fist.

To J.R. the idea that such a man might have anything to do with the murder of a teenage girl was, to use the phrase he intended to use should such a possibility be offered, "patently absurd."

"How many girls do you have working there at the factory, Mr. Frank?" Langford asked.

"About a hundred."

"And you handle the payroll?"

"Actually, Mr. Shiff pays the girls."

"Well, you were paying them on Saturday, weren't you?" Starnes asked, a sudden, accusatory note in his voice.

"Yes."

"What do you pay them, by the way?" Rogers asked.

"The girls make twelve cents an hour," Frank answered.

Black smiled. "What do you make, Mr. Frank?" he asked. He glanced at the other detectives. "In case I ever got interested in managing a pencil factory, I mean."

The men laughed. Frank didn't.

"My salary is sixty dollars a week," he said.

"And you say you've got a hundred girls working for you, Mr. Frank?" Langford asked.

"About a hundred, yes."

"That's a lot of girls," Starnes said. "All young, right?"

Frank gave a quick, jerky nod. "Most of them are young, yes."

"You like them that way?" Rogers asked. "Young?"

Frank looked at him silently.

"As employees, he means, Mr. Frank," Langford added softly.

Frank glanced about nervously. "I don't have any preference, really. As to age, It just happens that most of the girls are young. I think you would find that in any factory of this kind, that most of the girls are . . ."

"What about Mary Phagan?" Starnes interrupted. "When we went to your house, you said you didn't know who she was."

Frank tugged gently at his right cuff link. "At first, I didn't recognize the name."

"So you don't know the names of the people who work for you?" Rogers asked.

Frank allowed himself a quick, jittery laugh. "Well, there are so many . . ."

"A hundred, yes," Black said sharply. "A hundred girls."

Frank's eyes darted away, settled briefly on J.R.'s, then fled back to Newport Langford. "Once I saw her . . . Mary . . . I knew who she was. I mean, I recognized her." He adjusted the cuffs of his shirt unnecessarily, twisted his cuff links. "That it was Miss Phagan."

"And you remembered paying her on Saturday, is that right?" Rogers asked.

"Yes, she came to my office."

"On the second floor," Starnes said.

"That's right."

The men stared at him silently.

"She asked for her pay," Frank added. "I looked it up. The amount, I mean. How much I owed her. Then I gave her what she was due."

"And she left?" Starnes asked.

"Yes."

"And you stayed put," Black said.

"At my desk."

"For how long?" Rogers asked.

"At least two hours."

The questions and answers continued, J.R. listening idly, glancing out into the bull pen from time to time, hoping to see McCorkindale or some other uniform escort

Jim Conley into the room. He'd learned by then that Newt Lee was denying everything, claiming that the murder was being "put off" on him. He thought of the notes Craig Britt had found beside the body, the low, subliterate writing scrawled on them.

"Let's get back to Mary for a moment, Mr. Frank," Langford said.

Frank fingered a gold cuff link.

"Had she ever been in your office before?"

"Not that I recall."

"What about the other girls?" Starnes asked. "Were they in the habit of coming up to the second floor?"

Frank looked at Langford quizzically, then turned back to Starnes. "In the habit?"

"Did you bring these girls up to your office on a regular basis?" Black snapped.

"I never brought them up," Frank said.

"Well, they been seen up there," Rogers told him.

"To get their pay," Frank replied.

"Do they ever come up there just to see you?" Starnes asked.

"Me?"

"Pay a call, you might say."

"No."

"No girl ever comes up there alone?" Black asked doubtfully.

"To get her pay, she might," Frank said.

"Never for anything else?" Starnes asked.

Frank shook his head.

"How about Mary Phagan," Langford said. "Had Mary ever been in your office before yesterday afternoon, Mr. Frank?"

Frank's right hand moved from his lap to his left cuff link. "Not that I recall. No."

"Well, you would recall it, wouldn't you?" Starnes asked. "If she'd come up there before?"

"Not necessarily," Frank answered. "I mean, I have . . ."

"A hundred girls, yeah, we know," Black said sharply. He looked knowingly at the other men. "We've heard all about it."

Frank lowered his eyes, and for a moment J.R. tried to read the gesture. Embarrassment? Fear? Something else? The notes returned to him. He tried to imagine Conley writing them in the shadowy corner of the basement, hunched, ape-like, over Mary Phagan's dead body, dabbing the tip of the pencil on his thick red tongue, eyes rolling toward the ceiling as he tried to figure out exactly what he should "wright."

"You're not from around here, are you, Mr. Frank?"

It was Starnes going at him again.

"I was born in Texas," Frank said.

"Texas?" Black asked. "You don't sound like you're from Texas."

"My family moved to Brooklyn when I was a baby," Frank said. He offered a quick, nervous smile.

"My wife was born here in Atlanta, though. A native. Her father is head of the B'nai B'rith."

"What's that?" Starnes asked.

Frank's smile vanished. "An association."

"Of what?"

Frank grabbed his knees, squeezed. "Of Jews," he said, glancing about. "Of Jewish people."

Langford nodded softly. "How long did you live in Brooklyn, Mr. Frank?"

"Until I graduated from college."

"What did you study, may I ask?"

"Mechanical engineering."

J.R. felt something shift in his mind. Could the notes have been planted by someone else? Someone a lot smarter than Conley? Able to figure out a double insinuation, put the murder on an inferior being. Conley, by making it seem that he, Conley, had tried to implicate a second inferior being. Newt. Knowing all the time that Newt would never fit the bill, but that Conley would. J.R. smiled at the idea of such a scheme. Clever, he thought.

"Normally, you wouldn't have been at the factory on a Saturday, is that right, Mr. Frank?"

It was Mr. Langford asking, softly, politely, always adding, "Mr. Frank" at the end of it.

"No," Frank said. "I wouldn't have been there at all if it hadn't been raining."

"What's that?" Rogers asked.

"I'd planned to go to a baseball game with my brother-in-law."

Starnes smiled. "Baseball? You like baseball?"

Frank looked at him. "Why does that surprise you?"

Starnes' face turned grim. "Who was playing?"

Frank shifted slightly. "Well, the Atlanta team, I believe."

"The Crackers," Black said.

"Yes."

"Who were they playing?" Starnes asked. "Who were the Crackers playing yesterday?"

Frank was silent for a moment, then shook his head. "I don't. . . ."

Starnes smiled thinly. "Birmingham," he said. "The Birmingham Barons."

Frank shrugged. "I . . ."

Langford leaned forward, his eyes boring into Frank now. "Mr. Frank, one thing bothers me. Why did you call Newt Lee down at the factory on Saturday afternoon?"

Before he could answer, Starnes leaned forward. "After you'd left. Two hours after you'd left."

"I wanted to make sure everything was all right at the factory."

"Why wouldn't it be?" Rogers asked.

"Well, Newt is new at the factory, and so . . ."

"He was even newer last Saturday," Starnes said. "But you didn't call him then."

Frank shrugged. "I just wanted to check on things."

"On Mary Phagan?" Black asked.

Frank stared at him quizzically, one hand drifting toward the left cuff, tugging at the cuff link. "Mary Phagan? Why would I . . ."

"Maybe you wanted to find out if anybody had found her yet," Rogers asked starkly. "Is that why you called Newt?"

Frank shook his head. "Of course not," he said, then went on, sputtering. "I had no idea that anything had . . . that-that Miss Phagan was . . . no idea."

J.R. eased his weight from the wall, watching Frank's hands, something he'd noticed, the way Frank's slender, delicate fingers toyed with the gold cuff links each time he heard Mary Phagan's name. J.R. thought of the notes again, how cleverly they'd been constructed, pointing at guilt by pointing away from guilt, which pointed back to guilt again. He wondered if Conley could ever have hatched such a scheme. He was smart, but was he that smart? He considered both the nature and scope of Conley's intelligence, both his shrewdness and its limits. His shrewdness would inform him of his limits. Which meant, J.R. reasoned, that since Conley was smart, he'd know better than to get himself mixed up in a contest of wits with a mechanical engineer. He would know that he could never outsmart so superior a person. This, J.R. reasoned, was an argument that worked both ways. For just as surely, Leo Frank would know that he could outsmart Conley. This logic applied with telling force, J.R. mused, on the notes Britt had found beside the body. For although Conley would know that he could never hope to write like Leo Frank, Frank would no less clearly perceive that he, Frank, could quite easily imitate the crude sublanguage of such a brute as Jim Conley.

"You must admit, Mr. Frank, that that call is somewhat of a problem," Langford said.

Frank stared at him silently.

"It seems out of character, you see," Langford explained politely.

Frank's eyes took on a strange, animal agitation. "Out of character? In what way?"

"In that a man like you, Mr. Frank," Langford said, "if you'll permit me saying so"—he tapped the side of his head—"a man like you has a reason for everything he does."

Frank started to answer, but the door to Langford's office swung open suddenly, and Luther Rosser strode in.

"I'm Mr. Frank's lawyer," he declared. "There will be no more questioning of my client without my being present."

Langford stood up slowly, shook hands with Rosser, then let his gaze drift down to where Frank sat, completely still, in his chair. "You may go, Mr. Frank," he said. He smiled at Rosser. "I'll walk you to your car, Luther," he added brightly.

The detectives shifted about, muttering, then drifted away from Frank, giving him room to straighten himself, watching silently as he buttoned his coat, adjusted his tie. Then Frank turned and headed for the door, J.R. standing massively in his path, so that he slowed suddenly, as if a great stone had suddenly rolled into his path.

J.R. stood in place for only the briefest moment, then shifted to the right, cleared the way. "Thank you for coming in, Mr. Frank," he said.

Frank read something in his gaze. "I didn't kill Mary Phagan."

J.R. smiled. "Better straighten your cuff links," he said.

For an instant their eyes locked. Then Rosser took Frank's arm, urged him forward. "Let's go, Leo," he told him.

J.R. watched as the three men, Langford somewhat in the lead, made their way across the empty bull pen to the stairs. Once they'd gone through the double doors, become mere blurs behind its frosted glass, he stepped over to the window and looked out. A black car rested at the curb, its chrome fenders shimmering even in the gray light. Briefly, the three men stood in a tight circle, talking amicably. Then the conversation ended, and Rosser opened the car's back door to let Frank in.

The other detectives had joined J.R. at the window by then. "What do you think, J.R.?" Rogers asked.

J.R. turned from the window just as McCorkindale walked into the bull pen, Jim Conley at his side. He watched as McCorkindale led Conley to a chair, cuffed him to it, then walked away, leaving Conley alone, staring about. J.R. peered at him closely, noted the thick neck, the small, curled ears and popped brown eyes, the way, when he caught J.R. watching him, he offered up a wide, gap-toothed grin.

Very low, J.R. thought, as he turned back to the window, his gaze now on Leo Frank once again.

"Langford will ask you first," Starnes said. "It's probably up to you, J.R. If you say he's clear, he's clear."

Below, Frank stood for a moment in the clear, clean air, gazing about, as if in melancholy appreciation, like someone saying goodbye to something he'd never noticed before, but held precious now.

"Well?" Black asked. "Did Frank do it?"

Gold cuff links winked in the sunlight.

"What do you think, J.R.?"

Truth dawned as it always did in J.R.'s mind, clean and bracing, fresh as a bright new day.

"Dead sure," he said.

FATHERHOOD

W atching them from a distance, the way she rocked backward and forward in her grief, her arms gathered around his lifeless body, I could feel nothing but a sense of icy satisfaction, relishing the fact that both of them had finally gotten what they deserved. Death for him. For her, perpetual mourning.

She'd worn a somber gown for the occasion, her face sunk deep inside a cavernous black hood. She stared down at him and ran her fingers through his blood-soaked hair, her features so hideously distorted by her misery it seemed impossible that she'd ever been young and beautiful, or even felt delight in anything.

By then the years had so divided us and embittered me that I could no longer think of her as someone I'd once loved. But I *had* loved her, and there were times when, despite everything, I could still recall the single moment of intense happiness I'd had with her.

She'd been only a girl when we first met, the town beauty. Practically the only beautiful thing in the town at all, for it was a small, drab place set down in the middle of a desert waste. To find something beautiful in such a place was nearly miracle enough.

She was already being pursued by the local boys, of course. They were dazzled by her black hair and dark oval eyes, skin that gave off a striking olive glow. I yearned for her no less ardently than they, but I kept my distance.

Looking out my shop window, I would often see her as she swept down the street, heading toward the market, a large basket on her arm. Coming back, the basket now filled with fruit and vegetables, she'd sometimes stop to wipe a line of sweat from her forehead, her eyes glancing briefly toward the very window where I stood watching her, and from which I always quickly retreated.

The fact is, she frightened me. I was afraid of the look that might come into her eyes if she saw me staring at her, the pity, perhaps even contempt, for a portly, middle-aged bachelor who worked in a dusty shop, lived alone in a single musty room, had no prospects for the future, and who had nothing to offer a vibrant young woman like herself.

And so I never expected to speak to her or approach her in any way. To the extent that she would ever know me, it seemed certain it would be as the anonymous figure she sometimes noticed as she made her way to the market, a person of no consequence or distinction, as flat and featureless in her mind as the old stones she trod upon. My fate would be to watch her silently forever, see her life unfold from behind my shop window, first as a young woman hastening to the market, then as a bride strolling arm-in-arm with her new husband, finally as a mother with children following behind her, her beauty deepening with the years, becoming fuller and richer while I kept my post at the window, growing old and sickly, a ghostly, gray-haired figure whose life had finally added up to nothing more than a long and fruitless longing.

Then it happened. One of those accidents that make a perpetual mystery of life, that bless the unworthy and doom the deserving, and which give to all of nature the aspect of a flighty, cruel, and unloving queen.

One of my customers had tethered a horse to the post outside my shop. It was sleek and beautiful, and coming back from the market, the girl of my dreams stopped to admire it. First she patted its haunches. Then she moved up the twitching flanks to stroke its moist black muzzle. Finally, she fed it an ear of corn from the overflowing basket she'd placed at my feet.

"Is it yours?" she asked me as I came out the door, my arms filled with wood I used in my trade.

I stopped, astonished to see her staring at me, unable to believe that she'd actually addressed her question to me.

"No," I said. "It belongs to one of my customers."

She returned her attention to the horse, drawing her fingers down the side of its neck, twining her fingers in its long brown mane. "He must be very rich to have a horse like this." She looked at the wood still gathered in my arms. "What do you do for him?"

"Build things. Tables. Chairs. Whatever he wants."

She offered a quick smile, patted the horse a final time, then retrieved her basket from the street and sauntered slowly away, her brown eyes swinging girlishly in the afternoon light, her whole manner so casual and lighthearted that only a sudden burst of air from my mouth made me realize that during the time I'd watched her stroll away from me, I had not released a breath.

———◇———

I didn't talk to her again for almost three months, though I saw her in the street no less often than before. A young man sometimes joined her now, as beautifully tanned as she was, with curly black hair. He was tall and slender, and his step was firm, assured, the walk of a boy who had never wanted for anything, who'd inherited good looks and would inherit lots of money, the sort whose bright future is entirely assured. He would marry her, I knew, for he seemed to have the beauty and advantage that would inevitably attract her. For days I watched as they came and went from the market together, holding hands as young lovers do, while I stood alone, shrunken and insubstantial, a husk the smallest breeze could send skittering down the dusty street.

Then, just as suddenly, the boy disappeared, and she was alone again. There were other changes too. Her walk struck me as less lively than it had been before, her head lowered slightly, as I had never seen it, her eyes cast toward the paving stones.

That anyone, even a spoiled, wealthy youth, might cast off such a girl as she seemed inconceivable to me. Instead, I imagined that he'd died or been sent away for some reason, that she had fallen under the veil of his loss and might well be doomed to dwell within its shadows forever, a fate in one so young and beautiful that struck me as inestimably forlorn.

And so I acted, stationing myself on the little wooden bench outside my shop, waiting for her hour after hour, day after day, until she finally appeared again, her hair draped over her shoulders like shimmering black wings.

"Hello," I said.

She stopped and turned toward me. "Hello."

"I have something for you."

She looked at me quizzically, but did not draw back as I approached her.

"I made this for you," I said as I handed it to her.

It was a horse I'd carved from an olive branch.

"It's beautiful," she said, smiling quietly. "Thank you."

"You're welcome," I said and, like one who truly loves, asked nothing in return.

We met often after that. She sometimes came into my shop, and over time I taught her to build and mend, feel the textures and qualities of wood. She worked well with her hands, and I enjoyed my new role of craftsman and teacher. The real payment was in her presence, however—the tenderness in her voice, the light in her eyes, the smell of her hair—how it lingered long after she'd returned to her home on the other side of town.

Soon, we began to walk the streets together, then along the outskirts of the village. For a time she seemed happy, and it struck me that I had succeeded in lifting her out of the melancholy I had found her in.

Then, rather suddenly, it fell upon her once again. Her mood darkened and she grew more silent and inward. I could see that some old trouble had descended upon her, or some new one that I had not anticipated and which she felt necessary to conceal. Finally, late one afternoon when we found ourselves on a hill outside the village, I put it to her bluntly.

"What's the matter?" I asked.

She shook her head, and gave no answer.

"You seem very worried," I added. "You're too young to have so much care."

She glanced away from me, let her eyes settle upon the far fields. The evening shade was falling. Soon it would be night.

"Some people are singled out to bear a certain burden," she said.

"All people feel singled out for the burdens they bear."

"But people who feel chosen. For some special suffering, I mean. Do you think they ever wonder why it was them, why it wasn't someone else?"

"They all do, I'm sure."

"What do you think your burden is?"

Never to be loved by you, I thought, then said, "I don't think I have one burden in particular." I shrugged. "Just to live. That's all."

She said nothing more on the subject. For a time, she was silent, but her eyes moved about restlessly. It was clear that much was going on in her mind.

At last she seemed to come to a conclusion, turned to me, and said, "Do you want to marry me?"

I felt the whole vast world close around my throat, so that I only stared at her silently until, at last, the word broke from me. "Yes." I should have stopped, but instead I began to stammer. "But I know that you could not possibly . . . that I'm not the one who can . . . that you must be . . ."

She pressed a single finger against my lips.

"Stop," she said. Then she let her body drift backward, pressing herself against the earth, her arms lifting toward me, open and outstretched and welcoming.

Any other man would have leapt at such an opportunity, but fear seized me and I couldn't move.

"What is it?" she asked.

"I'm afraid."

"Of what?"

"That I wouldn't be able to . . ."

I could see that she understood me, recognized the source of my disabling panic. There seemed no point in not stating it directly. "I'm a virgin," I told her.

She reached out and drew me down to her. "So am I," she said.

I didn't know how it was supposed to feel, but after a time she grew so warm and moist, my pleasure in her rising and deepening with each offer and acceptance, that I finally felt my whole body release itself to her, quaking and shivering as she gathered me more tightly in her arms. I had never known such happiness, nor ever would again, since to make love to the one you love is the greatest joy there is.

For a moment we lay together, she beneath me, breathing quietly, the side of her face pressed against mine.

"I love you," I told her, then lifted myself from her so that I could see her face.

She was not looking at me, nor even in my direction. Instead, her eyes were fixed on the sky that hung above us, the bright coin of the moon, the scattered stars, glistening with tears as she peered upward to where I knew her thoughts had flown. Away from me. Away. Away. Toward the one she truly loved and still longed for, the boy whose beauty was equal to her own, and for whom I could serve as nothing more than a base and unworthy substitute.

———◦———

And yet I loved her, married her, then watched in growing astonishment as her belly grew day by day until our son was born.

Our son. So the townspeople called him. So she called him and I called him. But I knew that he was not mine. His skin had a different shade, his hair a different texture. He was tall and narrow at the waist, I was short and stocky. There could be no doubt that he was the fruit of other loins than mine. Not my child, at all, but rather the son of that handsome young boy she'd strolled the town streets with, and whose disappearance, whether by death or desertion, had left her so bereft and downcast that I'd tried to cheer her with a carved horse, walked the streets and byways with her, soothed and consoled her, sat with her on the far hillside, even made love to her there, and later married her, and in consequence of all that now found myself the parent and support of a child who was clearly not my own.

He was born barely six months after our night of love. Born weighty and full-bodied and with a great mass of black hair, so that it could not be doubted that he had lived out the full term of his nurture.

From the first moment, she adored him, coddled him, made him the apple of her eye. She read to him and sang to him, and wiped his soiled face and feet and hindquarters. He was her "dear one," her "beloved," her "treasure."

But he was none of those things to me. Each time I saw him, I also saw his father, that lank and irresponsible youth who'd stolen my wife's love at so early an age that it could never be recaptured by her or reinvested in me. He had taken the love she might have better spent elsewhere, and in doing that, he had left both of us impoverished. I hated him, and I yearned for vengeance. But he had fled to parts unknown, and so I had no throat to squeeze, no flesh to cut. In his stead, I had only his son. And thus I took out my revenge on a boy who, as the years passed, looked more and more like his youthful father, who had the same limber gait and airy disposition, a boy who had little use for my craft, took no interest in my business, preferring to linger in the town square, talking idly to the old men who gathered there, or wile away the hours by reading books on the very hillside where I'd made love to his mother, and who, even as I'd released myself into her, had slept in the warm depths of her flesh.

I often thought of that. The fact that my "son" had been inside her that night, that my own seed had labored to reach a womb already hardened against them. Sometimes, lost in such dreadful speculations I would strike out at him, using my tongue like a knife, hurling glances toward him like balls of flame.

"Why do you hate him so?" my wife asked me time after time during those early years. "He wants to love you, but you won't let him."

My response was always the same, an icy silence followed by a shrug.

And so the years passed, my mood growing colder and more sullen as I continued to live as a stranger in my own household. In the evening, I would sit by the fire and watch as a wife who had deceived me and a son who was not my son played games or read together, laughed at private jokes, and discussed subjects in which I had no interest and from whose content and significance I felt purposely excluded. Everything they did served only to heighten my solitary rage. The sound of their laughter was like a blade thrust in my ear, and when they huddled in conversation at the far corner of the room, their whispers came to me like the hissing of serpents.

During this time my wife and I had terrible rows. Once, as I tried to leave the room, she grabbed my arm and whirled me back around. "You're driving him from the house," she said. "He'll end up on the street if you don't stop it. Is that what you want?"

For once, I answered with the truth. "Yes, I do. I don't want him to live here anymore."

She looked at me, utterly shocked not only by what I'd said, but the spitefulness with which I'd said it. "Where do you expect him to live?"

I refused to retreat. "I don't care where he lives," I answered. "He's old enough to be on his own." There was a pause before I released the words I'd managed to choke back for years. "And if he can't take care of himself, then let his *real* father take care of him for a while."

With that, I watched as tears welled up in her eyes before she turned and fled the room.

But even after that, she didn't leave. Nor did her son. And so, in the end, I had to stay in the same house with them, live a life of silent, inner smoldering.

A year later he turned fifteen. He was nearly a foot taller than I was by then. He'd also gained something of a reputation as a scholar, a fact that pleased his mother as much as it disgusted me. For what was the use of all his learning if the central truth of his life remained unrevealed? What good all his command of philosophy and theology if he would never know who his real father was, never know where he'd gotten his curly black hair and lean physique, nor even that keenness of mind which, given the fact that he thought me his natural father, must have struck him as the most inexplicable thing of all?

But for all our vast differences of mind and appearance, he never seemed to doubt that I was truly his father. He never asked about other relatives, nor about any matter pertaining to his origins or birth. When I called him to his chores, he answered, "Yes, Father," and when he asked my permission, it was always, "May I, Father?" do this or that. Indeed, he seemed to relish using the word. So much so that I finally decided it was his way of mocking me, calling me "Father" at every opportunity for no other reason than to emphasize the point either that he knew I was not his father, or that he wished that I were not.

For fifteen years I had endured the insult he represented to me, my wife's deviousness, her false claim of virginity, the fact that I'd had to maintain a charade from the moment of his birth, claiming a paternity that neither I nor any of my neighbors believed to be genuine. It had not been easy, but I had borne it all. But with his final attempt to humiliate me by means of this exaggerated show of filial obedience and devotion, this incessant repetition of "Father, this" and "Father, that," he had finally broken the back of my self-control.

And so I told him to get out, that he was no longer welcome in my house, that no more meals would be provided, nor any bed for him to sleep in, nor a fire to warm him, nor clothes for his back.

We stood together in the backyard, he watching me silently while I told him all this. He'd grown a beard during that preceding few weeks, his hair had fallen to his shoulders, and he'd taken to going barefoot. "Yes, Father" was all he said when I finished. Then he turned, walked back into the house, gathered a few personal items in a plain cloth knapsack, and headed down the street, leaving only a brief note for his mother, its sneeringly ironic message clearly intended to render me one final injury, "Tell Father that I love him, and that I always will."

——◀◦▶——

I didn't see him again for eighteen years, though I knew that my wife maintained contact, sometimes even making long treks to visit whatever town he was passing through. She would return quite exhausted, especially in the later years, when her hair was gray and her once radiant skin had become so easily bruised that the gentlest pressure left marks upon it.

I never asked her about her trips, never asked a single question about how her son was doing. Nor did I miss him in the least. And yet, his absence never gave me the relief I'd expected. For it didn't seem enough, my simply throwing him out of the house. I had thought it might satisfy my need to get even with his father and my wife for blighting my life, forcing me to live a transparent and humiliating lie. But it hadn't.

Vengeance turned out to be a hungrier animal than I'd supposed. Nothing seemed to satisfy it. The more I thought of my "son," the more I got news of his various travels and accomplishments, heard tales of the easy life he had, merely wandering about, living off the bounty of others, the more I wanted to strike at him again, this time more brutally.

He had become quite well known by then, at least in the surrounding area. He'd organized a kind of traveling magic show, people said, and had invented an interesting patter to go along with his tricks. But when they went on to describe the things he said, it seemed to me that the "message" he offered was typical of the time. He was no different from the countless others who believed that they'd found the secret to fulfillment, and that their mission was to reveal that secret to the pathetic multitude.

I knew better, of course. I knew that the only happiness that is possible comes by accepting how little life has to offer. But knowing something and being able to live according to that knowledge are two different things. I knew that I'd been wronged, and that I had to accept it. But I could never put it behind me, never get over the feeling that someone had to pay for the lie my wife had told me, the false son whose very existence kept that lie whirling madly in my brain. I suppose that's why I went after him again. Just the fact that I couldn't live without revenge, couldn't live without exacting another, graver penalty.

It took me three years to bring him down, but in the end it was worth it.

———◁◦▷———

She never knew that I was behind it. That for the preceding three years I'd silently waged my campaign against him, writing anonymous letters, warning various officials that he had to be watched, investigated, that he said violent things, urged people to violence, that he was the leader of a secret society pledged to destroy everything the rest of us held dear. By using bits of information gathered from my wife, I kept them informed about his every move so that agents could be sent to look and listen. He was arrogant and smug, and he had his real father's confidence that he could get away with anything. I knew it was just a matter of time before he'd say or do something for which he could be arrested.

I did all of that, but she never knew, never had the slightest hint that I was orchestrating his destruction. I realized just how fully I had deceived her only a few minutes after they'd finally peeled her away from his dead body and taken it away to prepare for burial. We were walking down the hill together, away from the place where they'd hung him, my wife muttering about how terrible it was, about how brutally the mob had taunted and reviled him. Such people could always be stirred up against someone like our son, she said, a "true visionary," as she called him, who'd never had a chance against them.

I answered her sharply. "He was a fraud," I said. "He didn't have the answer to anything."

She shook her head, stopped, and turned back toward the hill. It was not only the place where they'd executed him, but also the place where we'd first made love, an irony I'd found delicious as they'd led him to the execution site, his eyes wandering and disoriented, as if he'd never expected anything so terrible to happen to him, as if he were like his real father, wealthy and irresponsible, beyond the fate of ordinary men.

A wave of malicious bitterness swept over me. "He got what he deserved," I blurted out.

She seemed hardly to hear me, her eyes still fixed on the hill, as if the secret of his fate were written on its rocky slope. "No one told me it would be like this," she said. "That I would lose him in this way."

I grasped her arm and tugged her on down the hill. "A mother is never prepared for what happens to her child," I said. "You just have to accept it, that's all."

She nodded slowly, perhaps accepting it, then walked on down the hill with me. Once at home, she lay down on her bed. From the adjoining room, I could hear her weeping softly, but I had no more words for her, so I simply left her to her grief.

Night had begun to fall, but the storm that had swept through earlier that day had passed, leaving a clear blue twilight in its wake. I walked to the window and looked out. Far away, I could see the hill where he'd been brought low at last. It struck me that even in the last moments of his life, he'd tried to get at me just one more time. In my mind I could see him glaring down at me, goading me in exactly the way he had before I'd kicked him out of the house, emphasizing the word *Father* when he'd last spoken to me. He'd known very well that this was the last time he'd ever talk to me. That's why he'd made such a production of it, staring right into my eyes, lifting his voice over the noise of the mob so that everybody would be sure to hear him. He'd been determined to demonstrate his defiance, his bitterness, the depth of his loathing for me. Even so, he'd been clever enough to pretend that it was the mob he cared about. But I knew that his whole purpose had been to humiliate me one last time by addressing me directly. "Father," he'd said in that hateful tone of his, "Father, forgive them, for they know not what they do."

NAMELESS STONES

My father was a doctor in the northern foothills of Alabama. He was a large, mild-mannered man who took great care with his patients, carefully explaining everything he did to them before he did it. By Depression standards, he had a well-heeled town practice which rarely ventured out into the mountain regions above our town.

Most of his patients were local businessmen and professionals. Yet, for all that, my father still lived in what seemed to me a state of perpetual crisis. Night and day were pretty much indistinguishable in our house. Babies had to be born when they were ready, and people hurt or frightened came to him for help regardless of the hour.

There weren't many nurses in those days, and so after my mother died young, while attempting to have a second child, it was up to me to assist my father, to boil the water and arrange the instruments, to light the lanterns and put out the heavy cotton gauze and bandages, and at times to press down hard on someone's arm or leg or chest to keep him from injurying himself while he thrashed about in pain.

In those days medicine was a muscular profession—even for a nine-year-old boy.

From time to time people from the rural areas would wander in, bringing their various sufferings to our door. I remember them well: large women in flour-sack dresses and men in soiled gray shirts. Their children seemed to be hardly dressed at all. They were brought only when their parents had to bring them, when they had been sick so long or so terribly that their parents had finally become frightened for them.

Often too late.

Often they died.

Billie Withers died. He was a small, thin boy of four or five. His hands had a certain female delicacy to them, very soft and pale. Sometimes now when I reach over to take my wife's hands, I remember his.

The Withers were mountain people. And that is not to say they were stubborn or independent. It is not just to say they held to a code of silence or endurance.

They were mountain people in the sense that mountain life was the only life they knew. The ridges and granite cliffs were their cosmos. They could not imagine a world beyond them.

That in Istanbul muezzins called the people to prayer from lofty minarets or in Paris women danced barebreasted upon ornate revolving stages or in India people worshipped a god with an elephant's head—it was not that these things were unknown to the Withers and their neighbors; they simply did not exist for them.

What existed was the mountains, and they lived within their limited reaches like flowers captured in a vase. The farthest ridge was for them a beach, and all which lay beyond it an unknown, unknowable sea.

John Withers brought his son Billie to our house on a cold December night. When I opened the door, he snatched his hat from his head and held it reverently in his hand. "Is Doctor Franklin here?" he asked.

He was wearing a pair of denim overalls over a faded yellowish shirt with a frayed collar. His face was drawn, worried. He looked as though he had lost a good deal of sleep.

"Yes, sir," I said.

Mr. Withers nodded shyly at the small boy cradled in his arms. "Mah boy's in bad shape, I thank," he said.

I stepped back and asked him to come in.

He hesitated, started to move, then drew back as if his boots had rooted to the porch. "I hate to trouble you so late."

I opened the door a bit farther. "It's all right. I'll get my father. Come on in."

Mr. Withers stepped through the door into the foyer and glanced timidly left and right. "I shore do hate to put you to this trouble."

"Just stay here," I said. "My father will be out in a minute."

I walked quickly back to the kitchen where my father was having one of his hasty late-night snacks. He had gotten used to never going to bed before midnight during the early days of his practice and had never been able to readjust his hours.

"Who's at the door?" he asked.

"A man with a little kid."

He pushed himself away from the table, still looking longingly at a half-eaten piece of chicken. "All right, go make sure my office is straightened up."

I ran to my father's examining room and began putting things in their proper places. He never had been a neat man, and his proper material element seemed to be a kind of usable but ultimately incomprehensible chaos.

His medicine bottles were deposited randomly throughout the office, and his instruments lay about on table tops, shelves and chairs. It was as if the logic which science brought to his mind had been imposed upon some older and less ordered beast.

Billie was whimpering slightly when Mr. Withers brought him into the room.

"Just lay him down there," my father said, and Mr. Withers gently placed Billie on the black cushioned table in the middle of the room.

My father stepped over to the table and began loosening the patchwork quilt covering Billie. "How long has he been sick?" he asked.

"'Bout a week," Mr. Withers said. "He ain't been no better in a while."

My father brought one of the kerosene lanterns over to the table for light.

"Hi there," he said brightly when Billie opened his eyes and stared languidly at the light.

"You're not feeling too well, I guess," my father said, comfortingly.

Billie squinted and tried to answer.

"No, no," my father said, "just rest still. We'll have you out playing ball in no time."

Billie's eyes closed slowly. He had a small, beautiful face, a mountain boy's face, open and unvarnished as the day he was born. Beneath the glaze, his eyes seemed to be greenish with spots of brown. His hair was light brown streaked with blond. His skin was stretched tight against his cheek bones. In the lantern light it looked as smooth and shiny as unpainted porcelain.

"You treat him at all?" my father asked Mr. Withers.

"I dist wrapped 'im up and kep' 'im by the far," Mr. Withers said. He thought a moment, then added: "Mah wife's people come over and prayed fer 'im."

My father tugged gently at Billie's chin, slowly prying open his mouth. He peered in for a moment, delicately pressing down on Billie's tongue with a depressor. He sniffed his breath then listened to his heart.

I watched my father carefully and saw a slight wincing of his eyes. I had seen that look before, a tiny drawing together of the eyebrows and narrowing of the eyes. It was so subtle a gesture I doubted any but me had ever detected it.

It meant Billie Withers was most likely dying.

Mr. Withers watched my father closely. One of his hands nervously fingered the carpenter's loop in his overalls while the other rhythmically squeezed his crumpled gray hat.

Finally, my father turned to him. "Is your wife at home?"

"She's dead," Mr. Withers said. He continued to stare at Billie.

"I didn't catch your name, I don't believe."

"Withers. John Withers."

My father walked over to the medicine chest and took out a bottle of dark-colored serum. He filled a hypodermic needle with a large dosage.

"Your boy has diphtheria, Mr. Withers," he said. "Have you ever heard of that?"

Mr. Withers nodded. "Can you hep 'im?"

"Well, this medicine is supposed to do some good. Your boy has a pretty advanced bad case right now. This medicine sometimes has some bad things about it. Most of the time it's all right though. I think we'd better go ahead and use it."

"Dist do what you can fer 'im," Mr. Withers said. "I'd 'preciate it."

Billie's body rustled gently on the table, and Mr. Withers' lips parted as if his own breath were tied to the boy's.

My father smiled. "Could be he'll be playing with his brothers and sisters in a couple of days," he said.

"Naw," Mr. Withers said. "He's mah onliest kid." He took a deep breath and exhaled slowly. "He took sick all of a sudden."

My father held up the hypodermic so Mr. Withers could see it clearly. "I'm going to give him the shot now. It won't hurt him." He turned and quickly injected the antitoxin directly into Billie's veins.

"Can I take 'im home now?" Mr. Withers asked.

"No, I think you better not. He's pretty tired. He needs to rest. We'll let him sleep, see how he is in the morning. To tell you the truth, there's nothing to do but wait."

Mr. Withers nodded. "Awright."

My father turned back to Billie and ran his fingers through the boy's hair. "Fine boy." He circled his index finger gently around Billie's ear as he sometimes did mine.

"Could I stay with 'im?" Mr. Withers asked.

My father bundled Billie up again and lifted him into his arms. "There's plenty of room for both of you."

"I don't want to be no trouble."

"Plenty of room," my father repeated. "Come on, I'll show you."

Mr. Withers seemed to smile, and I could see the jagged, brownish teeth his closed lips had hidden. His face seemed softer now, less lined and pitted. The lantern light gave it an orange hue, making it look as if it had been carved out of the reddish clay of the hill country.

"Eddie, go get me an extra blanket," my father said to me.

I brought the blanket into the back bedroom and watched as my father laid Billie on the bed. He listened to his heart once again, then folded the blanket double and tucked it delicately around Billie's body.

"We'll keep him nice and warm," he told Mr. Withers.

Mr. Withers took the edge of the blanket and pulled it over Billie's chin. "When he gits in bed, he goes all the way under the covers. Even covers up his head."

"Smart boy," my father said lightly. "That heats the bed faster."

"Dist all of a sudden took sick," Mr. Withers muttered. "Dist clumb in mah lap and took sick."

"I'll bring a cot in for you," my father said.

Mr. Withers rubbed his eyes. "Naw, that's awright. I couldn't git no sleep. I'll dist set in that chair there."

"You ought to get some rest."

Mr. Withers shook his head. "Naw, thank you."

"Well, I'll sit up with you awhile," my father said. "I haven't been sleeping very well lately, anyway."

"Now don't go to no more trouble on 'count of me," Mr. Withers said insistently, drawing back from this last courtesy as if too much generosity could never be repaid.

My father pulled another chair up and sat down near Billie's bed. "No trouble," he said. "Have a seat yourself, Mr. Withers."

"Can I sit up, too?" I asked.

"For a while," my father said.

Billie moved gently under the covers and drew his small fist up near his lips. "Wife's people prayed fer 'im," Mr. Withers muttered. He paused, thinking. "I ain't a churchgoer."

My father tilted back in the oak rocker. "You know, they'll come a time when all of these childhood diseases will be gone. Little boys like your son here'll never have to worry about them. Tremendous progress is being made." He shook his head with wonderment. "Tremendous progress."

Mr. Withers continued to stare at Billie. "Bible says that the sins of the father are visited on the son," he said after a moment.

My father leaned forward and looked intently at Mr. Withers. "It's just a disease. Nothing else."

Mr. Withers took a handkerchief from his back pocket and wiped his mouth. "I never was a churchgoer."

"Believe me," my father said, "that has nothing to do with it. Don't worry yourself about it."

"My sister-in-law said that one time her uncle worked on Sunday and his little girl got sick. Crippled her. For life."

Billie's eyes fluttered open for a moment then closed. My father got up and listened to his heart. He glanced at Mr. Withers then at me. "Eddie, maybe you'd better get on to bed now," he said softly.

I stood up. "Good night, Mr. Withers."

"Thank you for your hep, boy," Mr. Withers said. He moved to tip his hat, realized it was squeezed tight in his hand and simply nodded. "I 'preciate it."

In the room next door I could hear my father and Mr. Withers talking quietly, but it was hard to make out exactly what they were discussing. At times I could hear words individually spoken—a yes here, a no there, Billie's name. Food and drink were offered and refused. I expected my father to leave after a while, but he never did. When the first morning light filtered through my window, I could still hear the slow, heavy tone of his voice. It sounded like a distant horn struggling through the fog.

Sometime during the night, Billie Withers died. I saw Mr. Withers out my window when I woke up. He was leaning against a tree, one leg gently pawing at the ground. He was facing away from me, but I could tell by the slump of his shoulders, by the way that his head hung forward, that the worst had happened.

"The boy died," my father said when I walked into the kitchen.

"I thought so," I said. "I saw Mr. Withers out in the yard."

"He needs some time to be alone. We'll be taking the body home this morning."

"Us?"

"Yes. Mr. Withers was on foot. He walked down here last night."

"All the way from up the mountain?"

My father broke an egg into the fry pan. "Only way he had."

After breakfast Mr. Withers gathered Billie in his arms, and we drove them up the mountain road to home. Except for giving a few directions, Mr. Withers did not say much. He sat in the back seat, sometimes staring out the window, sometimes watching Billie's face as if he were hoping for some sudden sign of life, a tremble in the lips or a pulse beneath the eyes.

For the whole noisy, jostling trip, he cradled Billie in his arms, supporting the back of his head like you would a newborn infant's.

The scene in the back of our Model A has always been to me the real *Pietá*, stark and beautiful as brown, wind-severed corn, unsoftened by blue light, unadorned, unsanctified, unknown.

Billie Withers was buried two days later in an unvarnished wooden coffin. You could hear the muffled sound of his body bumping against the sides as the men lifted him onto their shoulders and carried him to the cemetery behind the Mountain View Church of Christ.

It was a cold, overcast day. A small breeze fluttered the pages of the hymnals the people used to sing a farewell hymn. Their voices did not soar like the town choir I was used to. They sang in a flat, featureless monotone like ghosts rooted to earth, bound to it by invisible wires. The old people hugged themselves, holding their coats close about them, and the children watched the bleak ritual of Billie's burial with patient, respectful eyes.

A final prayer was said, and then the small congregation filed silently out of the cemetery. A few of the older ones lifted their collars against the wind.

Only Mr. Withers remained. He stepped over to my father and shook his hand. "You didn't have to come," he said. "Thank you."

"I'm sorry I couldn't help him."

Mr. Withers wiped a film of moisture and grit from his eyes. "Maybe it was meant to be."

"Someday it'll be different," my father said firmly. "We'll find the answers to these things."

Mr. Withers nodded, allowing my father's distant faith to pass without argument. "Well, thank you for what you done," he said.

He walked a few feet away, picked up a large, flat stone and sunk it into the ground at the head of Billie's grave. Then he took a small one and placed it carefully at the foot. He stood for a moment, staring at the grave, then clapped the dust from his fingers and walked away.

I looked curiously at the two stones. "Are those tombstones?" I asked. In the town cemetery they were made of marble.

"It's the way they mark the grave," my father said.

"But they don't even say anything, even a name."

"Poor people," my father said quietly.

He took my hand, and we began walking toward our car. The clouds to the east gathered behind us, gray and dense and invulnerable like the mysteries of God.

NEVERMORE

My father's last request was that I bring him a book. We had not been close, or even very much in communication, since the day my mother left him. Over the years, the many years, my anger with him had not abated. But in his final days, I'd decided to offer him at least an occasion for atonement, despite the fact that he'd never given any indication that he had anything for which he felt the need to atone. At times I'd even felt my presence in his hospital room reduced to that of a Shabbas goy, performing servile tasks like turning on a light or adjusting the volume on the television that hung opposite his bed.

"I'm a rabbi," I reminded him sternly one afternoon when my lowly status in his eyes became particularly irksome.

"So was I," my father said. "Almost."

Almost? I didn't think so. For although he'd been a rabbinical student in his youth, he'd later chosen Columbia over Yeshiva, and from there gone on to the life of a liberal arts professor, complete with pipe, tweed jacket, and, as I'd been told, an occasional mention in scholarly magazines.

"Poe," he said one Friday afternoon when the sun was setting and I was hurrying to leave.

"Poe?" I asked.

"The poems," my father said. "There's a volume of them somewhere around the house."

He'd been in the hospital for several days by then, suffering from the usual infirmities of old age, though this time with the added problem of pneumonia. His breathing was labored, and he seemed generally exhausted, not at all the vibrant man who'd daily escorted me into his study, whipped a book from the shelf, and taught me the classics and ancient history.

"Bring it on Monday," he added with a tired wave of the hand.

I recalled my father as a quick discarder of old books, always on the lookout for the latest edition, so when I got around to the latest humble task he'd asked of me, I found it surprising that his Poe was an old volume with yellowed, crumbling pages, a book that had the present look of my father, once sturdy and tightly bound, but now tattered beyond repair.

It had been nearly fifty years since I'd entered my father's study, but I found the look of it quite at one with the man himself. From the time he'd first left the Lower East Side, he'd been a "modern" man, with high, upwardly mobile ambitions. The glass-topped desk seemed perfectly in keeping with his character, as did the sleek leather chair with its gleaming chrome legs. There was a flatscreen monitor and an ergonomic keyboard, and just to the right, an iPod stood perkily in its white plastic stand.

I shook my head at the sheer predictability of it all. How fitting that this was where my father did his thinking, beneath halogen lights, with the silvery louver blinds open to reveal a neat, suburban lawn. For he was not at all the somber black-clothed scholar I thought myself to be, a man of prayers and fasting, immersed in the Torah, not in some lengthy study of imagery in *Lolita*. The fact is, we'd gone in completely opposite directions, and because of that my father's existence now seemed transparently thin to me, the man himself a cellophane soul, utterly without mystery, his life a story without twists or turns, one that surely would have proven an unfit subject for the inventor of the detective story.

"Why Poe?" my wife asked when, after my return home, I showed her the book my father had requested I bring him on Monday morning.

"I don't know," I answered. "He taught Poe only that last summer."

My wife covered her head and prepared to light the Shabbat candles. "Maybe that's what's on his mind," she said.

I shrugged. "If so, it's too late to make amends."

He took a severe turn for the worse two days later, so that when I arrived at the hospital that morning, I found him barely the shadow of the man I'd left the Friday before. He'd clearly been given something, as my mother had in her last hours. Like her, he'd been unable to speak coherently, though he appeared to be fully conscious. After offering my usual terse greeting I brought the book within view, showed him the spine. "The book you wanted," I said. "Poe." I drew a chair up to his bedside. "I thought I might read a few of the poems to you."

He stared at the book with what seemed the quiet affection and admiration he had once offered me, but which I had long ago rejected and continued to reject.

"So, let's begin." I flipped past the melancholy visage of the author, the title page, the table of contents, to the first poem in the volume. "'Alone,'" I said like a speller cautious to follow the rules of the bee, pronouncing the word before defining it.

> *From childhood's hour I have not been*
> *As others were; I have not seen*
> *As others saw; I could not bring*
> *My passions from a common spring.*

My father's eyes darted about, and for a moment he seemed disoriented.

"You're in Room 1213," I told him. "Clark Memorial."

He squinted hard, like a man trying to bring something small into focus.

"Shtorm," he said, then much more clearly, "Storm."

"Storm?" I asked, glancing at the poem again, now focused on the last line I'd read, *I could not bring my passions from a common spring.*

"Summer storm." One hand rose and floated out and away, like a boat into vastness, and his gaze went to the middle distance.

"What summer storm?" I asked.

He seemed frustrated, grasping at words, determined to say something that either his weakness or the drugs prevented him from saying. "Poe," he said softly, then louder, more emphatically, "teaching Poe."

So my wife had been right. He *was* thinking about the idyllic three months during which he'd held forth on Poe, often in a little arbor beside Lake Montego, deeply shaded and oddly romantic, with his few exchange students gathered around him.

He struggled to speak again, faltered, then blurted almost vehemently, "*Shiksa.*"

I stared at him, stunned. For although before leaving him my mother had often used the old world languge of her parents—*meshugana*, for a crazy person, *mitzvah* for a good deed—my father had shunned Yiddish entirely, thought it fit only for comedy, and even then for the lowest kind. He'd even corrected my English when it slipped into what he called "foreignness." "In America we don't 'close' the light, Alex," he'd once said to me when I'd inadvertently used one of my mother's phrases. "We 'turn it off.'"

"*Shiksa*?" I asked. "Since when do you . . ."

"Summer, storm, Poe," my father said, connecting all three words, though without giving the connection any decipherable meaning.

"Summer, storm, Poe," he repeated, his tone urgent, as if he were searching through his vast vocabulary, riffling through the great cabinet of his mind for some purloined letter that would explain his life.

"*Shiksa*," he said, paused, searched, then added, "Sarah."

Sarah was my mother's name, and my father's use of *shiksa* and *Sarah* in such juxtaposition immediately returned me to the climactic scene that seemed most disastrously to connect them. I saw my mother and father in our car on a particularly stormy day, though one whose wind and rain I'd hardly have noticed had the car come only part way up the drive and then stopped without going into the garage. Abruptly stopped, with a jolt, as if someone had stomped the brakes.

"I was seven when we left," I said softly, remembering that dreadful, life-altering day, the thudding rain, my mother's anger a quite different storm, one that had proven far more devastating to the landscape of my youth.

But this was a disturbing recollection, fraught with old rage, and so I quickly returned to Poe's poem and began to read again:

From the same source I have not taken
My sorrow; I could not awaken
My heart to joy at the same tone;
And all I loved, I loved alone.

"Never," my father said. "I would never."

He appeared to be rambling now, his focus less clear. I barely acknowledged what he said. For despite the effort, I found myself still fixed in place at the second-floor window, the little boy I'd once been, peering down into the chasm of adulthood, where the family car halted at the rim of the house and my mother dashed out into the rain while my father sat behind the weeping glass, listening to the *thump, thump, thumping* of what I had considered since that storm-tossed day to be his profoundly selfish heart.

"You are . . ." my father murmured. "You are . . ."

The callous heart of a man my mother had left more than fifty years before, left to his suburban house and big-shot college professorship, left and taken me with her and returned us both to the din of New York, where we'd lived with my grandmother in a crowded neighborhood, Ludlow Street. My mother hence known to all as Surala, speaking Yiddish to the vendors and shopkeepers, using her hands when she spoke, covering her head and lighting the candles for Friday night prayers—*Baruch Atah Adonai*—and from which world, with my father far away, his visits growing more infrequent, I had made my way unfathered into the world.

"Alexander," my father said.

It was the name he'd chosen for me, a conqueror of worlds, and certainly inappropriate for the rabbi I was, with a synagogue on Sixth Street and a little apartment in Stuyvesant Town.

"I'm Ezra," I reminded him starkly. "I've been Ezra since . . ." I stopped, already irritated by my little visit to the past. "Ezra is my name."

My name because it was the name called out in the synagogue, the middle name that had been chosen by my mother, and so, as I saw it, forever my name, shouted in greeting by the pickle sellers on Essex Street and the tradesmen of Delancey, by the old people in the park and the young people in the handball courts, my name to my grandmother, carried on breath laced with herring, past lips crumbed with latkes, my name to all the "old world" my father had despised and back to which my mother, in her brokenness, had fled, and by which she had again been made whole, and so the world I had embraced as my world too, this island, where storms also raged, of course, but always amid the anchorage of the old traditions and blood relations and neighborhood bonds, faith and family and friends.

"Ezra," I repeated, like a man raising a proud old flag.

My father drew in a trembling breath but said nothing, so I returned to the poem:

> *Then—in my childhood, in the dawn*
> *Of a most stormy life—was drawn*

From every depth of good and ill
The mystery which binds me still:

He poked his chest with a single finger, eyes glaring. "I am the father," he said with an odd fury, like a man declaring an ancient and inalienable right.

I looked up from the page and considered this "father" of mine, a man who had renounced so many holy things—the language of his youth, the history of his people; severed so many sacred bonds—marriage, fatherhood—lost so much that was precious and irrecoverable that he seemed the victim of some monstrous theft, though I knew *he* was the thief. And with that thought I returned to the window, the storm, my mother dashing through the tearing wind, my father silent behind the wheel, his eyes following the rhythmic pulse of the windshield wipers, listening to the *thump, thump, thump,* as I imagined it, of his own telltale heart.

My father's lips twitched and jerked as he tried to speak, now moving his head from side to side as if laboring to shake the words from his mind.

"Lenore," he said finally.

Lenore.

So now, I thought bitterly, now when he could no longer speak whole sentences easily, when he was too weak to sustain anything resembling conversation, when he had to rely on some kind of associative code, now, at the very border of coherence, after all the damage he had done, the terrible betrayal he had inflicted upon my mother, now, now, my father finally wanted to talk about her, this young girl who'd listened as he'd pontificated about Poe, this *shiksa* whose life had ended early and violently, in the throes of a passion my father held in the very contempt he'd expressed so starkly in that storm-tossed car, the cruelty of which had caused my mother to stomp the brake. *For God's sake, Sarah, she's just a girl.*

Her name, this "girl," was Lenore. She had pale skin and yellow hair, just like the Lenore of Poe's poem, and it was easy for me to imagine just how beguilingly my father had used her name's connection to Poe's pining love song as a way of seducing her, how he must have asked her to linger in the arbor after the other students had left, sat with her in that deep shade, quoted Poe to her, made her believe that she was "fair and debonair," like the lost Lenore.

I never knew how my mother found out about her, or learned any of the details of her immediate response, save the terrible admission that had caused her to stomp the brake of the family car as it had drawn up to the garage that stormy afternoon.

"Lenore?" I said to him now. "Spare me."

My father closed his eyes, but I could see them moving about beneath the lids, back and forth and up and around like following a flying bit of paper.

I lifted the volume toward him. "Poe," I said firmly, since my mother had made me promise never to speak of my father's betrayal, a promise it had been easy to keep since my father had never seemed to feel the slightest guilt concerning Lenore, or my mother's abrupt departure, or even the loss of me. The deep grudge I'd nursed against him, a fire from which he'd finally drawn away, with fewer and fewer visits and phone calls until my bar mitzvah, and after that, as if freed by my full embrace of the faith he had so fully rejected, I could without guilt, and almost as if commanded, hold him in a searing contempt I had made since my thirteenth year no effort to conceal.

After that rupture, my father's phone calls had dwindled into nothing, and we'd retreated into our vastly separate worlds, he the strolling luminary of a grassy college campus, I, a familiar figure on the old fabled streets, Essex and Orchard and Rivington, well known and not without honor in the little *shtetl* of my life.

I pointed to the open book of Poe's poems. "Shall I go on?"

My father eased back wearily and closed his eyes like a man defeated in some final purpose.

I returned to the poem and began to read:

> *From the torrent, or the fountain . . .*
> *From the red cliff of the mountain,*

I stopped, but why? What did I want? I knew quite well what it was, of course. I wanted an apology. I wanted my father to tell me that he was truly, deeply sorry not only for what he'd done, but for what he was. I wanted him to tell me that he had been wrong in everything, wrong in all he had rejected and in all he had taken up, that his every guiding thought had been wrong, that he'd been wrong at every turn, wrong about my mother, wrong about me, and coldly, cruelly wrong in destroying our family over some nothing of a girl, this poor, distraught Lenore.

He'd gone to her that same wind-driven afternoon. I'd watched from the second-floor window, oddly transfixed by what I'd already seen, and so held by the curious prospect of what would happen next. My father sat, as if in mute suspension, behind the wheel of his spanking-new sedan, while downstairs I could hear my mother as she strode from room to room, her feet pounding angrily against the hardwood floors below.

And so I was still at the window when my father came to his conclusion, slapped the gear into reverse, and guided the car back out of the driveway, where he stopped again, though only briefly, perhaps turning some final notion over in his mind before pressing down upon the accelerator and heading east, toward Lake Montego.

Meanwhile, as the public record later showed, Lenore had also journeyed out into the storm, her body wrapped in an old wool coat, her yellow hair bound in a red scarf, her shoes protected by her very English "wellies," and so, by all accounts, a careful young woman, careful with her clothes, her shoes, her modest ambitions, careful with the feelings of her family and her female reputation, careful in everything, as it had later seemed, save in what she'd let herself feel for my unfeeling father.

My father had driven directly to the little bungalow Lenore shared with two other English girls, one named Betty, who later told authorities that he looked angry when he came for Lenore, and one named Dotty, who said he looked flustered and a little confused. Neither had known of their summer roommate's relationship with the man they called Professor Green before he'd shown up at their door, though they had noticed a change in Lenore, a nervousness they'd attributed to anxiety about her studies. Her long hours of walking in the nearby woods had taken a toll, they thought, as well as her late hours at the college library. Then, in an instant, it had all come clear to them, they said, Lenore crying, distraught, pulling on her coat and galoshes, barging out into the storm, my father banging at their bungalow door a few minutes later, the motor left running in his car, windshield wipers thumping in the rain.

Back on Giddings Street, of course, I'd heard a very different thumping, first my mother as she climbed the stairs, and after that, the soft thump of her suitcase as she tossed it onto the bed. I didn't hear the whisper of clothes hastily packed, however, and so I had no idea of anything so dire as the decision she'd made until she suddenly called to me from the hallway, "Alexan . . ." A pause. "Ezra."

And so everything had changed.

But less for me, as it turned out, than for yellow-haired Lenore.

She had gone to the boathouse, and when I think of her at the moment my father found her there, I imagine her sitting, wrapped in her own arms, eyes red with crying, the very picture of a broken-hearted young woman, innocent and naïve, the perfect prey for a man such as my father. Professor Green, smooth-tongued, erudite, with his prized Phi Beta Kappa key dangling from his watch chain, this great, learned warship of a man whose seductive wiles the small craft that was Lenore surely could not have resisted.

For as I later learned, Mary Lenore Leeds was a lowly working-class girl, little more than a scullery maid, who'd won a summer semester in America at a Liverpool dance hall. She'd picked my father's course on Poe from the great variety of academic offerings open to her because, according to Betty and Dotty, she'd liked penny dreadfuls, read them by the score, and thus had been surprised when Professor Green disparaged them. But they had had a talk, Lenore told her roommates, and after that . . .

I had always had trouble imagining the "after that" of my father and Lenore, not because it is almost impossible for children to imagine a parent in the act of sexual congress, but because my father had never seemed physical at all. He'd been all brain to me, all books and learning, all authority and judgment, a secular father of biblical proportions. Aristotle, in the inflated way he seemed to think of himself, to my Alexander.

But he had hardly turned out to be that sort of sage, a sad fact of life my mother had often made clear. Rather, he was the phony *ba'al torah* who'd lacked wisdom to hold his family together, a vain and haughty man, always *farputst*, with his scholar's key and gold watch, a puffed-up *feinshmeker* who'd fallen victim to his own exalted image of himself, taken advantage of a young girl and *murdered her*, to use my mother's phrase, though she well knew he had not done that.

Or had he?

For murder, or at least the possibility of it, was surely what I'd taken from the newspaper accounts of Lenore's death. I'd been a freshman at Yeshiva before I'd actually read them, warned away from the story by my mother, who had seemed to bury the details of her leaving my father in a deep grave of secrecy. But after reading the newspaper stories, the notion of foul play had lingered in my mind, so that once, after watching that sad and frightening scene from *A Place in the Sun* where an ambitious, social-climbing Montgomery Clift rows the distraught, pregnant working girl who loves him out onto a lake and murders her for his own advantage, I'd felt a dreadful question circle through my mind. For Lenore had died like that, drowned after somehow falling over the side of the small boat she'd taken out onto storm-tossed Lake Montego. But had she gone alone? Or had my father gone with her, done what he had to do in order to get rid of this inconvenient little strumpet, once he had himself dismissed as "just a girl"?

It would be easy, I thought, to kill someone who could be dismissed with the very words my father had said in the car that afternoon, words that had always seemed to me the true mark of his cruelty. And if he had done nothing, why had he never gained high position at the college, never become a dean or head of his department, never soared up and up as he'd no doubt expected to soar?

I felt the darkest suspicion of my life rise like a gush of bile in my throat.

"Did you kill her?" I blurted suddenly. "Did you kill that . . . pregnant *shiksa*?"

My father's eyes burst open.

"Is that why my mother left you?" I demanded. "Not just that you *schtupped* that girl, but that you killed her?"

My father began to kick and pull at his sheets, twisting his body and jerking his head. But none of his contortions summoned the slightest pity in me. Let him kick and toss about forever, I thought. Let the dogs of his conscience, the ghosts of all he'd so recklessly thrown aside, even the ghost of Alexander, that little boy who'd loved him so, let them all have their way with him, chew his flesh and drink his blood and break his bones, and finally reduce him to the same dust his betrayal had made of my childhood adoration of him.

Then quite suddenly he stopped, and with what seemed a mighty effort, said "*Nischt mein.*"

I'd seen other people revert to words and phrases they'd not used since childhood, people long rooted in the suburbs who'd abruptly returned, as it were, to the *shtetl* of their parents or grandparents, the blasted villages and charred ghettos of a vanished Poland. But this latest of my father's reversions to Yiddish seemed less natural than calculated, perhaps his way of mocking me.

"I've always wondered if you did it," I said. "If you rowed her out on that lake, into that storm, with nobody around, no other boats on the lake, just rowed her out into that storm and tossed her over the side."

My father jerked his head to the right in a way, it seemed to me, a guilty man would turn from his chief accuser.

I waited briefly, thinking he might look back toward me, actually address the accusation I'd made, but he didn't, and after a time I went back to Poe's poem.

> *From the sun that round me rolled*
> *In its autumn tint of gold,*

My father released a long, weary breath. "*Farblonschet.*"

It was an almost comic term for being confused, and again I wondered if he was mocking me.

"So, you're confused?" I asked, now determined to speak to him only in English, as if Yiddish were my language, and could never be his, Yiddish and all that clung to it just another worthy thing he'd brutally renounced, a language that was like me, something he never visited or called, a Yid to this anti-Semite, a piece of *dreck*.

My father twisted around and pointed to me with a shaky finger.

"So, I'm the one who's confused?" I laughed. "About what?"

My father began to squirm, so that I could see the effort he was making, the energy it took for him to say simply, "Sarah . . . never . . . never . . ." A jumble of sounds followed, none of them decipherable. Then, quite clearly, though with failing strength, he said, "Not mine."

He saw that I had no idea what he was talking about, and with a labored movement reached out for the book.

I handed it to him, and watched as he thumbed through the pages until he found the one he wanted, then tapped the title of the poem.

"Lenore?" I asked. "Lenore wasn't yours?"

But that was absurd, I thought, *for had not my mother discovered the whole sordid business, confronted him with it in the car on that stormy afternoon, heard his heartless dismissal of Lenore*—She's just a girl.

"What about the baby?" I asked.

He shook his head furiously, clearly and forcefully denying that Lenore's baby was his.

"Not mine," he repeated. He twisted about, lips fluttering, so that it seemed to me that he was using up the last dwindling energy of his life in some final effort to communicate what I'd once hoped might be an apology, but which was clearly something else.

I leaned forward. "Whose then?"

Again my father seemed to take up a mighty struggle, hands jerking at the sheets, legs ceaselessly moving, lips twisting, his eyes darting about, until they settled on the window, emphatically settled, like a pointing finger.

I looked out the window, the grounds empty save for the young workman in the distance pushing a lawnmower, and made a wild guess.

"Joey?" I asked. "The kid who mowed our lawn?"

My mother had always called him the Shabbas goy. He'd mowed the lawn and trimmed the shrubbery and done anything else that she required any time one of her girlhood friends from the old neighborhood visited, always frumpily dressed, these now middle-aged women with herring on their breath, and the old country in their voices and memories of their but recently slaughtered kindred still hanging like hooks in their hearts.

"Joey?" I asked again.

My father nodded fiercely.

I recalled Joey O'Brian as tall and very skinny, with bad skin and bad teeth, a red-headed young man I'd once found staring quizzically at the little mezuzah my mother had tacked up at the front door of our house—*Waz zat, guv*? When I'd answered, he'd chuckled and shaken his head, so distant from it all, not just Jewishness, but college towns, professors and their little boys, rooms lined with books.

"You're saying it was Joey . . . the father?"

My father nodded and his eyes brightened like a man who at last understood.

"You and Lenore never . . ."

My father shook his head firmly.

But if this were true, why had my mother ever left him? I wondered. If my father had not even had a fling with Lenore, much less murdered her, then why had my mother packed her bags, called me Ezra, dragged me from the house, and taken me back into the world of her father and out of the world of mine?

I leaned forward and stared into my father's eyes. "Why did my mother leave that day?"

My father shook his head, as if surrendering to silence, to something that would forever remain confused.

"Why?" I repeated.

He closed his eyes, and in the silence that settled over us, I took the book from his hand, returned to the earlier poem, and read its final stanza softly.

> *From the lightning in the sky*
> *As it passed me flying by*
> *From the thunder and the storm*
> *And the cloud that took the form*
> *(When the rest of Heaven was blue)*
> *Of a demon in my view*

My father opened his eyes slowly, and to my surprise, they were glistening. He nodded toward the book, and I could see that he was too tired to speak, that the haze of drugs or perhaps even the weight of his own impending death was exerting an irresistible power over him. Still, he seemed to think that somewhere in those tattered pages he might find words he could no longer say.

And so I began to turn the pages again, through poem after poem, past "Annabel Lee" and "The Bells," on to "The Raven," and past it, too, until I reached "Tamarlane," and heard my father groan, a signal it seemed to me, that this was the poem he wanted.

I put my finger on the first line, and looked at him. He shook his head and so I continued down the page, his head shaking and shaking until I reached these lines:

> *The rain came down upon my head*
> *Unshelter'd—and the heavy wind . . .*

"The day of the storm," I said.

My father nodded and smiled, and it seemed to me at that strange moment we suddenly returned to the world we had once known and loved, he the patient teacher, I the adoring student.

And so I recited the events of that day as I had come to know them.

"Okay, the day of the storm. You and my mother came home. You were in the car together."

He nodded again, paused briefly, like a man gathering up his strength, then with the greatest effort he had made so far, he spoke.

"Argument," he said in a tone very different from the one my mother had described or my bitter imagination had created and which seemed to embody the depth of his loss.

"But it was not over Lenore? Is that what you're saying?"

My father nodded excitedly, as if to say, *Yes, yes.*

"Over what?" I asked.

My father seemed even now reluctant to tell me what had passed between him and my mother on that stormy afternoon. His pause was long and thoughtful before he lifted his hand and pointed to me.

"Me?" I asked. "You were arguing about me?"

The old twinkle came into his eye, as when I'd been a boy in his study, he my devoted teacher, often speaking to each other through verses quoted from the great poems of the West, whole conversations carried out in that erudite yet oddly intimate way.

"What about me?" I asked.

My father pointed to the book and began waving his hand, a gesture that sent me flipping back through the pages of Poe's poems, slowly one by one, thinking that he sought a poem, perhaps certain lines.

I'd almost returned to the first of those poems by the time he groaned, a signal I should stop.

I looked at him, utterly puzzled. "Why here?" I asked. "It's a blank page."

He struggled to speak, but only a few slurred sounds came out, nothing I could make sense of.

"It's a blank page," I repeated. "There's nothing on it."

My father shook his head violently, clearly denying what I had just told him.

"There's nothing on this page but the number," I told him.

He nodded fiercely.

I looked at the number. "Thirteen?"

Again he nodded wildly. Then with great effort he said, "Never . . . never."

So the argument had been about me, had something to do with the number thirteen, something my father associated with the word never.

"*Me*," I said, turning the first of my father's words over in my mind. "*Thirteen. Never.*"

And suddenly I knew what he was struggling to tell me, what the number thirteen could only mean in relation to me, and what he must have said to my mother about that relationship.

"You told my mother that you'd never allow me to be bar mitzvahed?" I asked.

He nodded solemnly.

I saw my mother as I knew she must have been at that moment in her life, that moment as they sat with the rain thudding around them, and she saw him fall like a man through a gallows floor, fall utterly from the world they'd once shared, the rabbinical student my father had once been, how deeply my mother had expected to live as a rabbi's wife, and how different that life had become, the suburban life of a professor's wife, unrooted and unmoored, as she must have thought of it, though never, never as utterly lost to all that was holy until that moment in the storm when my father had effectively told her, and no doubt bluntly, that her son was not to be a Jew.

I could only imagine the utter fury with which my mother must have received this final proof of my father's demonic secularism, proof once and for all of how arrogantly he had discarded the sacred values, how deeply and irrevocably he had dismissed the commandments and commentaries, the centuries of accumulated wisdom, and with it the fierce need she must have felt to flee this dead-souled modernist, this despiser of ritual, of all the honored customs, this pragmatist who believed in quick solutions, in getting rid of obstacles, this radical assimilationist who was ashamed of his own people, felt no pity for the great heaps of European dead, who wished only to throw off the yoke of the past, make himself new . . . this *American*.

He eased himself back into his pillow and released a long deflating breath, so that I saw that even now he remained unsure of what he'd done, whether he'd been right or wrong, even though this seemed to matter less to him at that moment than what I would do with this strange revelation.

He tried to speak, but nothing came. So after a moment, and with what appeared to be the very last of his vital force, he motioned for me to give him the volume of Poe. I rose and sat on the bed beside him, holding the book open and turning the pages until he found the verse he wanted.

"Be that word our sign in parting, bird or fiend,"
  I shrieked, upstarting—
"Get thee back into the tempest and the Night's
  Plutonian shore!
Leave no black plume as a token of that lie thy
  soul hath spoken!
Leave my loneliness unbroken!—quit the bust above
  my door!
Take thy beak from out my heart, and take thy
  form from off my door!"
Quoth the Raven, "Nevermore."

He placed a single, trembling finger on that final word and looked up at me quizzically, no doubt wondering, perhaps quite desperately, if I could intuit the question his eyes asked. *Will you answer as the Raven does? Will you refuse to abandon me?*

For my answer, I took the book from his hands and read the last stanza of Poe's great poem:

And the Raven, never flitting, still is sitting, still
  is sitting
On the pallid bust of Pallas just above my chamber
  door;

I looked up and saw that he understood.

"I won't leave you alone," I assured him.

Had the world been less the thing it is, and more the thing we wish it were, then my father would have recovered, and we would have had a few more years to work out the long confusion of our lives, come to graceful terms, so that by the time his death at last arrived, I would have been a truly loving son, he a loving father, the two of us at last in some accord with what he had done, and I had done, what he was and what I became. But it was too late for that, as I could see by his waning strength. And so I accepted what the Talmud teaches, that no act can be wholly undone. *But then, "The Raven" teaches that, too,* I thought, and so I returned to it and began to read to my father again, this time from the beginning, a land both dark and dreary rising before me as I read, that place denied all true atonement, and where, as Poe so darkly knew, each second turns Forever into Nevermore.

RAIN

Battery Park

A burst of light releases the million eyes of the rain, glimpsing the Gothic towers in dark mist, falling in glittering streams of briefly reflected light, moving inland, toward the blunt point of the island, an outbound ferry as it loads for the midnight run.

So like I said before, it ain't like she has long, you know?

Yeah, mon. She just hangin' on now.

Rain streaks down the ferry's windows where the night riders sit in yellow haze—Toby McBride only one among them, single, forty-two, the bowling alley in trouble, thinking of his invalid mother on Staten Island, money

leaching away, watching her Jamaican nurse, such big black
hands, how easy it would be.

I figure you could use twenty grand, right?

Twenty, huh?

The rain falls on intrigue and conspiracy, trap doors,
underground escape routes, the crude implements of quick get-
aways. It collects the daily grime from the face of the Custom
House and sends it swirling into the vast underground drains
that empty into the sea. Along the sweep of Battery Park it
smashes against crumpled cigarette packets, soaks a broken
shoelace, flows into a half-used tube of lipstick, drives a young
woman beneath a tattered awning, blond hair, shoulder-length,
with a stuck umbrella, struggling to open it, a man behind her,
sunk in the shadows, his voice a tremble in the air.

You live in this building?

Long, dark fingers still the umbrella, curl around its
mahogany handle.

Name's Rebecca, right?

The rain sees the fickle web of chance meetings, the grid
of untimely intersections, lethal fortuities from which there
will be no escape. A million tiny flashing screens reflect sti-
lettos and box cutters, switchblades and ice picks, the snubnosed barrel that stares out from its nest of long dark fingers.

Don't say a word.

Off West Street the rain falls on the deserted pit of the
ghostly towers, and moves on, cascading down the skeletal

girders of the new construction, then further north to Duane Street, thudding against the roof of an old green van.

So, when you get here, Sammy?

Don't worry. I'll be there.

Eddie squeezes the cell phone, glances back toward the rear of the van, speakers, four DVD players, two car radios, a cashmere overcoat, a shoebox of CDs, some jewelry that might be real, the bleak fruit of the hustle.

I need you here now, man.

You that hyped?

Now, man.

In the gutters, the rushing rain washes cigarette butts and candy wrappers, a note with the number 484 in watery ink, a hat shop receipt, a prescription label for Demerol. It washes down grimy windshields and as it washes, sees the pop-eyed and the drowsy, the hazy and the alert, Eddie scratching his skinny arms, Detective Boyle in the unmarked car a block away playing back the tape, grinning at his partner as he listens to the voices on the ferry.

We got McBride dead to rights, Frank.

A laugh.

That fucking Jamaican. Jeez, does he know how to work a wire.

At Police Plaza, the wind shifts, driving eastward, battering the building's small square windows, a thudding rumble that briefly draws Max Feldman from the photographs on his desk, Lynn Abercrombie sprawled across the floor of her Tribeca apartment, shot once with a snubnosed .38, no real clues save the fact that she lay on her back with a strand of long blond hair over the right eye, maybe done by a fan of Veronica Lake, some sick aficionado of the noir.

The rain falls upon the tangle of steel and concrete, predator and prey. It slaps the baseball cap of Jerry Brice as he waits for Hattie Jones, knowing it was payday at the all-night laundry, her purse full of cash. It mars Sammy Kaminsky's view of Dolly Baron's bedroom window and foils the late-night entertainment of a thousand midnight peepers.

On Houston Street, it falls on people drawn together by the midnight storm, huddled beneath shelters, Herman Devane crowded into a bus refuge, drunk college girls all around him, that little brunette in the red beret, her body naked beneath her clothes, so naked and so close, the touch so quick, so easy, to brush against her then step back, blame it on the rain.

Lightning, then thunder rolling northward over Bleecker Street, past clubs and taverns, faces bathed in neon light, nodding to the beat of piano, bass, drums, the late-night riff of jazz trios.

Ernie Gorsh taps his foot lightly beneath the table.

Not a bad piano.

Jack Plato, fidgeting, toying with the napkin beneath his drink, a lot on his mind, time like a blade swinging over his head.

Fuck the piano. You hear me, Ern? 484 Duane. A little jewelry store. Easy. I cased it this afternoon.

Ernie Gosch listens to the piano.

Jack Plato, slick black hair, sipping whiskey, cocksure about the plans, the schedule, where the cameras are.

Paulie Cerrellos is backing the operation. A safe man is all we need. Christ, it's a sure thing, Ern.

Ernie Gorsh, gray hair peeping from beneath his gray felt hat, just out of the slammer, not ready to go back.

Nothing's ever sure, Jack.

It is if you got the balls.

It can't if you don't got the brains.

Plato, offended, squirming, a deal going south, Paulie will be pissed. No choice now but to play the bluff.

Take it or leave it, old man.

Ernie, thinking of his garden, the seeds he's already bought for spring, seeds in packets nestled in his jacket pocket, thinking of the slammer too, how weird it is now, gangs, Aryans, Muslims, fag cons raping kids in the shower, deciding not to go back.

Sorry, Jack. Rising. *I got a bus to catch.*

The eyes of the rain see the value of experience, the final stop of crooked roads. It falls on weariness and dread, the iron bars of circumstance, the way out that looks easy, comes with folded money, glassine bags of weed, tinfoil cylinders stuffed with white powder, floor plans of small jewelry stores, with Xs where the cameras are.

At 8th Street and Sixth Avenue, Tracey Olson leaves a cardboard box on the steps of Jefferson Market. Angelo and Luis watch her rush away from inside a red BMW boosted on Avenue A, the rain thudding hard on its roof.

You see that?

Wha?

That fucking girl.

What about her?

She left a box on the steps there.

What about it?

That all you can say, whataboutitwhataboutit?

Luis steps out into the rain, toward the box, the tiny cries he hears now.

Jesus. Jesus Christ.

On 23rd, the rain slams against the windows of pizza parlors and Mexican restaurants, Chinese joints open all night.

Sal and Frankie. Sweet and sour pork. Moo goo gai pan.

So, the guy, what'd he do?

What they always do.

He ask how old?

I told him eighteen.

Sal and Frankie giggling about the suits from the sub-
urbs, straight guys who dole out cash for their sweet asses
then take the PATH home to their pretty little wives.
Where was he from?
Who cares? He's a dead man now.
That plum sauce, you eatin' that?

At Broadway and 34ᵗʰ, the million eyes of the rain smash
against the dusty windows of the rag trade, Lennie Mack at
his desk, ledgers open, refiguring the numbers, wiping his
moist brow with the rolled sleeves of his shirt, wondering
how Old Man Siegelman got suspicious, threatening to
call in outside auditors, what he has to do before that call
is made . . . do for Rachel, and the two kids in college,
do because it was just a little at the beginning. Jesus, two
hundred fifty thousand now. Too much to hide. He closes
the ledger, sits back in his squeaky chair, thinks it through
again . . . what he has to do.

From Times Square, the gusts drive northward, slanting
lines of rain falling like bullets, exploding against the black
pavement, the cars and buses still on Midtown streets, Jaime
Rourke on the uptown 104, worrying about Tracy, what
she might do with the baby, seated next to an old guy in a
gray felt hat fingering packets of garden seed.
So I guess you got a garden.
My building has little plots. A smile. *My daughter thinks I
should plant a garden.*

Eddie Gorsh sits back, relaxed, content in his decision, grateful to his daughter, how, because of her, there'll be no more sure things.

Daughters are like that, you know. They make you have a little sense.

Near 59th and Fifth, a gust lifts the awning of the San Domenico. Dim light in the bar. Bartender in a black bolero jacket.

Amanda Graham. Martini, very dry, four olives. Black dress, sleeveless, Mikimoto pearls. Deidre across the small marble table. Manhattan. Straight up.

Paulie's going to find out, Mandy.

Amanda sips her drink. *How?*

He has ways.

A dismissive wave. *He's not Nostradamus.*

Close enough. And for what? Some nobody.

He's not a nobody. He plays piano. A nice gig. On Bleecker Street.

My point exactly.

Amanda nibbles the first olive. *What do you really think Paulie would do?*

Deidre sips her drink.

Kill you.

Amanda's olive drops into the crystal glass, ripples the vodka and vermouth. The smooth riffs of Bleecker Street grow dissonant and fearful.

You really think he would?

Over the nightbound city, the rain falls upon uncertainty and fear, the nervous tick of unsettled outcomes, things in the air, motions not yet completed. At 72nd and Broadway, it sweeps along windows coiled in neon, decorated with bottles of ale and pasted with green shamrocks.

Captain Beals. Single malt scotch. Glenfiddich. Detective Burke with Johnny Walker Black. A stack of photographs on the bar between them. Fat man. Bald. 3849382092.

This the last one?

Yeah. Feldman thinks it's a long shot, but the guy lives in Tribeca, and it seems pretty clear the killer lives there too.

A quick nod.

His name is Harry Devane. Lives in Windsor Apartments. Just a couple buildings down from Lynn Abercrombie. Four blocks from Tiana Matthews. Been out four years.

What's his story?

He works his way up to it by flashing, or maybe just rubbing against a girl. You know, in the subway, elevator, crap like that.

Then what?

Then he . . . gets violent.

How violent?

So far, assault. But pretty bad ones. The last time, the girl nearly died. He got seven years.

Ever used a gun?

No.

A sip of Glenfiddich.

Then he's not our man.

At 93rd and Amsterdam, the rain sweeps in waves down the tavern window, Paulie Cerrello watching Jack Plato step out of the cab, taking a sip from his glass as Plato comes through the door, slapping water from his leather jacket.

Fucking storm. Jesus.

So? Gorsh?

I showed him everything. The whole deal.

And?

He ain't in, Paulie. He's scared of the slammer.

Paulie knocks back the drink, unhappy with the scheme of things, some old geezer scared of the slammer, the whole deal a bust.

So what now, Paulie? You want I should get another guy?

A shake of the head.

No, I got another problem.

He nods for one more shot.

You know my wife, right?

The rain sees no way out, no right decision, nothing that can slow the encroaching vise. It falls on bad judgment and poor choice and the clenched fists of things half thought through. At Park and 104th, it slaps against a closing window, water on the ledge dripping down onto the bare floor.

Shit.

Leaves it.

Phone.

Yeah?

Charlie, it's me. Lennie.

This fucking storm flooded my goddamn apartment. Water all over the fucking floor.

Listen, Charlie. I need to borrow some cash. You know, from the guy you . . . from him.

A hard laugh.

You barely got away with your thumbs last time, Lennie.

But I made good, that's all that matters, right?

How much?

Twenty-five.

Charlie thinks. Old accounts. Too many of them. Past due. Lots of heavy leaning ahead. And if the leaning doesn't work, and somebody skips? His neck in a noose already.

So what about it, Charlie?

Not a hard decision.

No.

The rain sees last options, called bluffs, final scores, silenced bells, snuffed candles, books abruptly closed. At Broadway and 110th, the windshield wipers screech as they toss it from the glass.

Listen to that, will ya?

Yeah, what a piece of shit.

A fucking BMW, and shit wipers like that.

Might as well be a goddamn Saturn.

The box shifts slightly on Luis's lap.

I think it's taking a crap, Angelo.

So?

So? What if it craps through the box?

It won't crap through the box.

Okay, so it don't. What we gonna do?

I'm thinking.

You been thinking since we left the Village.

So what's your idea, Luis? And don't say cops, because we ain't showing up at no cop-house with a fucking stolen car and a baby we don't know whose it is.

A leftward glance, toward a looming spire.

A church. Maybe a church.

The rain falls on quick solutions, available means, a way out that relieves the burden. It falls on homeless shelters and SROs and into the creaky, precariously hanging drains of old cathedrals.

At 112th and Broadway, a blast of wind hits as the bus' hydraulic doors open.

Eddie Gorsh rises.

Good luck with the garden.

A smile back at the kid.

Thanks.

I got a daughter, too.

Then take care of her, and maybe she'll take care of you.

Out onto the rain-pelted sidewalk, head down, toward the building, Edna waiting for him there, relieved to have him back, the years they have left, a road he's determined to keep straight. This, he knows, will make Rebecca happy, and that is all he's after now.

The rain moves on, northward toward the Bronx, leaving behind new beginnings, things learned, lessons applied. At 116th and Broadway, Jamie Rourke steps out into the million, million drops, thinking of Tracey and his daughter, how he shouldn't have said what he said, made her mad, determined to call her now, tell her how everything is going to be okay, how it's going to be the three of them against the world, a family.

The rain falls on lost hopes and futile resolutions, redemptions grasped too late, fanciful solutions. At 116th and Broadway, it falls on Barney Siegelman as he steps out of a taxi, convinced now that his son-in-law is a crook, news he has to break to his wife, his daughter, the whole sorry scheme of things unmasked. He rushes toward the front of his building, feels the rushing tide up the sidewalk to Our Lady of Silence, where a cardboard box lies beneath a ruptured drain, a torrent gushing from its cracked mouth, filling the box with water, then over its sodden sides and down the concrete stairs, flooding the sidewalk with the stream that splashes around Siegelman's newly polished shoes. He shakes his head again. Tomorrow he'll have to have them shined all over again. He peers toward the church, the stairs, the shattered drain pipe, the overflowing box beneath it. Disgusting, he thinks, the way people leave their trash.

THE FIX

I t could have happened anytime, on any of my daily commutes on the Crosstown 42. Every day I took it at eight in the morning, rode it over to my office on Forty-second and Lex, then back again in the evening, when I'd get off at Port Authority and walk one block uptown to my place on Forty-third.

It could have happened anytime, but it was a cold January evening, a deep winter darkness already shrouding the city at six P.M. Worse still, a heavy snow was coming down, blanketing the streets and snarling crosstown traffic, particularly on Forty-second Street, where the Jersey commuters raced for a spot in the Lincoln Tunnel, clotting the grid's blue veins as they rushed for the river like rabbits from burning woods.

I should tell you my name, because when I finish with the story, you'll want to know it, want to check it out, see if I'm really who I say I am, really heard what I say I did that night on the Crosstown 42.

Well, it's Jack. Jack Burke. I work as a photographer for Cosmic Advertising, my camera usually focused on a bottle of perfume or a plate of spaghetti. But in the old days, I was a street photographer for the *News*, shooting mostly fires and water main breaks, the sort of pictures that end up on page 8. I had a front page in '74, though, a woman clinging with one hand to a fire escape in Harlem, her baby dangling from the other hand like a sack of potatoes. I snapped the button just as she let go, caught them both in the first instant of their fall. That picture had a heart, and sometimes, as I sat at my desk trying to decide which picture would best tempt a kid to buy a soda, I yearned to feel that heart again, to do or hear or see something that would work like electric paddles to shock me back to my old life.

Back in those days, working the streets, I'd known the Apple down to the core, the juke joints and after-hours dives. I was the guy you'd see at the end of the bar, the one in a rumpled suit, with a gray hat on the stool beside him. It was my seed time, and I'd loved every minute of it. For almost five years not a night had gone by when I hadn't fallen in love with it all over again, the night and the city, the Bleecker Street jazz clubs at three a.m. when the smoke is thick and the riffs look easy, and the tab grows like a rose beside your glass.

Then Jack Burke married an NYU coed named Rikki whose thick lips and perfect ass had worked like a Mickey Finn on his brain. There were lots of flowers and a twelve-piece band. After that the blushing bride seemed to have another kid about every four days. Jack took an agency job to pay for private schools, and that was the end of rosy tabs. Then Jack's wife hitched a ride on some other guy's star and left him with a bill that gave Bloomingdale's a boner. The place on Eighty-fifth went back to the helpful folks at Emigrant Savings, and Jack found a crib on West Forty-third. Thus the short version of how I ended up riding the Crosstown 42 on that snowy January night in the Year of Our Lord 2000.

The deepest blues, they say, are the ones you don't feel, the ones that numb you, so that your old best self simply fades away, and you are left staring out the window, trying to remember the last time you leaped with joy, laughed until you cried, stood in the rain and just let it pour down. Maybe I'd reached that point when I got on the Crosstown 42 that night. And yet, I wasn't so dead that the sight of him didn't spark something, didn't remind me of the old days and of how much I missed them.

And the part I missed the most was the fights.

I'll tell you why. Because all the old saws about boxing are true. There's no room for ambiguity in the ring. You know who the winners and the losers are. There, in that little square, under the big light, two guys put it all on the line, face each other without lawyers or tax attorneys. They stare at each other without speaking. They are stripped even of words. Boxers don't call each other names. They don't wave their arms and posture. They don't yell, Hey, fuck you, you fucking bastard, you want a piece of me, huh, well, come and get it, you fucking douche bag . . . while they're walking backward, glancing around, praying for a cop. Boxers don't file suit or turn you in to the IRS. They don't subscribe to dirty magazines in your name and have them mailed to your house. They don't plant rumors about drugs or how maybe you're a queer. Boxers don't come at you from behind some piece of paper a guy you never saw before hands you as you step out your front door. Boxers don't drop letters in the suggestion box or complain to your boss that you don't have what it takes anymore. Boxers don't approach at a slant. Boxers stride to the center of the ring, raise their hands, and fight. That was what I'd always loved about them, that they were nothing like the rest of us.

Even so, I hadn't seen a match in the Garden or any-where else for more than twenty years when I got on the Crosstown 42 that night, and the whole feel of the ring, the noise and the smoke, had by then drifted into a place within me I didn't visit anymore. I couldn't remember the last time I'd read a boxing story in the paper or so much as glanced at *Ring* magazine. As a matter of fact, that very night I'd plucked a *Newsweek* from the rack instead, then tramped onto the bus, planning to pick up a little moo shoo pork when I got off, then trudge home to read about this East

Hampton obstetrician who'd given some Jamaican bedpan jockey five large to shoot his wife.

Then, out of the blue, I saw him.

He was crouched in the back corner of the bus, his face turned toward the glass, peering out at the street, though he didn't seem to be watching anything in particular. His eyes had that look you've all seen. Nothing going on, precious little coming out. A dead, dull stare.

His clothes were so shabby that if I hadn't noticed the profile, the gnarled ear and flattened nose, I might have mistaken him for a pile of dirty laundry. Everything was torn, ragged, the scarf around his neck riddled with holes, bare fingers nosing through dark blue gloves. It was the kind of shabbiness that carries its own odor, and which urban pioneers inevitably associate with madness and loose bowels. Which, on this bus packed to the gills, explained the empty seat beside him.

I might have kept my distance, might have stared at him a while, remembering my old days by remembering his, then discreetly stepped off the bus at my appointed stop, put the whole business out of my mind until I returned to work the next morning, met Max Groom in the men's room and said, Hey, Max, guess who was on the Crosstown 42 last night? Who? Vinnie Teague, that's who. Irish Vinnie Teague, the Shameful Shamrock. Mother of God, he's still alive? Well, in a manner of speaking.

And that might have been the end of it.

But it wasn't.

You know why? Because, in a manner of speaking, I was also still alive. And what do the living owe each other, tell me this, if not to hear each other's stories?

So I muscled through the crowd, elbowing my way toward the rear of the bus while Irish Vinnie continued to stare out into the fruitless night, his face even more motionless when looked upon close up, his eyes as still as billiard balls in an empty parlor.

The good news? No smell. Which left the question, Is he nuts?

Language is a sure test for sanity, so I said, "Hey there."

Nothing.

"Hey." This time with a small tap of my finger on his ragged shoulder.

Still nothing, so I upped the ante. "Vinnie?"

A small light came on in the dull, dead eyes.

"Vinnie Teague?"

Something flickered, but distantly, cheerlessly, like a candle in an orphanage window.

"It's you, right? Vinnie Teague?"

The pile of laundry rustled, and the dull, dead eyes drifted over to me.

Silence, but a nod.

"I'm Jack Burke. You wouldn't know me, but years ago I saw you at the Garden."

The truth was I'd seen Irish Vinnie Teague, the Shameful Shamrock, quite a few times at the Garden. I'd seen him first as a light heavyweight, then later, after he'd bulked up just enough to tip the scales as a heavyweight contender.

He'd had the pug face common to boxers who'd come up through the old neighborhood, first learned that they could fight not in gyms or after-school programs but in barrooms and on factory floors, the blood of their first opponents soaked up by sawdust or metal shavings in places where no one got saved by the bell.

It was Spiro Melinas who'd first spotted Vinnie. Spiro had been an old man even then, bent in frame and squirrelly upstairs, a guy who dipped the tip of his cigar in tomato juice, which, he said, made smoking more healthy. Spiro had been a low-watt fight manager who booked tumble-down arenas along the Jersey Shore, or among the rusting industrial towns of Connecticut and Massachusetts. He'd lurked among the fishing boats that rocked in the oily marinas of Fall River and New Bedford, and had even been spotted as far north as coastal Maine, checking out the fish gutters who manned the canneries there, looking for speed and muscle among the flashing knives.

But Spiro hadn't found Vinnie Teague in any of the places that he'd looked for potential boxers during the preceding five years. Not in Maine or Connecticut or New Jersey. Not in a barroom or a shoe factory or a freezing cold New England fishery. No, Vinnie had been right under Spiro's nose the whole time, a shadowy denizen of darkest Brooklyn who, at the moment of discovery, had just tossed a guy out the swinging doors of a women's shelter on Flatbush. The guy had gotten up, rushed Vinnie, then found himself staggering backward under a blinding hail of lefts and rights, his head popping back with each one, face turning to pulp one lightning fast blow at a time, though it had been clear to Spiro that during all that terrible rain of blows, Vinnie Teague had been holding back. "Jesus Christ, if Vinnie hadn't been pulling his punches," he later told Salmon Weiss, "he'd have killed the poor bastard with two rights and a left." A shake of the head, Spiro's eyes fixed in dark wonderment. "I'm telling you, Salmon, just slapping him around you might say Vinnie was, and the other guy looked like he'd done twelve rounds with a metal fan."

Needless to say, it was love at first sight.

And so for the next two years Spiro mothered Vinnie as if he were a baby chick. He paid the rent and bought the groceries so Vinnie could quit his prestigious job as a bouncer at the women's shelter. He paid for Vinnie's training, Vinnie's clothes, Vinnie's birthday cake from Carvel, an occasion at which I was present, my first view of Irish Vinnie Teague. He was chewing a slab of ice cream cake while Spiro looked on, beaming. Snap. Flash. Page 8 over the lead line, UP-AND-COMER BREAKS TRAINING ON HIS 24TH.

He'd continued upward for the next four years, muscling his way higher and higher in the rankings until, at just the moment he came in striking distance of the title, Irish Vinnie had thrown a fight.

There are fixes and there are fixes, but Irish Vinnie's fix was the most famous of them all.

Why?

Because it was the most transparent. Jake LaMotta was Laurence Olivier compared to Vinnie. Jake was at the top of the Actors Studio, a recruiting poster for the Strasburg Method, the most brilliant student Stella Adler ever had . . . compared to Vinnie. Jake LaMotta took a dive, but Irish Vinnie took a swan dive, a dive so obvious, so awkward and beyond credulity, that for the first and only time in the history of the dive, the fans themselves started swinging, not just booing and waving their fists in the air, not just throwing chairs into the ring, but actually surging forward like a mob to get Vinnie Teague and tear his lying heart out.

Thirty-seven people went to Saint Vincent's that night, six of them cops who, against all odds, managed to hustle Vinnie out of the ring (from which he'd leaped up with surprising agility) and down into the concrete bowels of the Garden where he sat, secreted in a broom closet, for more than an hour while all hell broke loose upstairs. Final tab, as reported by the *Daily News*, eighty-six thousand dollars in repairs. And, of course, there were lawsuits for everything under the sun so that by the end of the affair, Vinnie's dive, regardless of what he'd been paid for it, had turned out to be the most costly in boxing history.

It was the end of Vinnie's career, of course, the last time he would ever fight anywhere for a purse. Nothing needed to be proven. The *Daily News* dubbed him the "Shameful

Shamrock" and there were no more offers from promoters. Spiro cut him loose and without further ado Vinnie sank into the dark waters, falling as hard and as low as he had on that fateful night when Douggie Burns, by then little more than a bleeding slab of beef, managed to lift his paw and tap Vinnie on the cheek, in response to which the "Edwin Booth of Boxers," another *Daily News* sobriquet, hit the mat like a safe dropped from the Garden ceiling. After that, no more crowds ever cheered for Vinnie Teague, nor so much as wondered where he might have gone.

But now, suddenly, he was before me once again, Irish Vinnie, the Shameful Shamrock, huddled at the back of the Crosstown 42, a breathing pile of rags.

"Vinnie Teague. Am I right? You're Vinnie Teague?"

Nothing from his mouth, but recognition in his eyes, a sense, nothing more, that he was not denying it.

"I was at your twenty-fourth birthday party," I told him, as if that were the moment in his life I most remembered rather than his infamous collapse. "There was a picture in the *News*. You with a piece of Carvel. I took that picture."

A nod.

"Whatever happened to Spiro Melinas?"

He kept his eyes on the street beyond the window, the traffic still impossibly stalled, angry motorists leaning on their horns. For a time he remained silent, then a small, whispery voice emerged from the ancient, battered face. "Dead."

"Oh yeah? Sorry to hear it."

A blast of wind hit the side of the bus, slamming a wave of snow against the window, and at the sound of it Irish Vinnie hunched a bit, drawing his shoulders in like a fighter . . . still like a fighter.

"And you, Vinnie. How you been?"

Vinnie shrugged as if to say that he was doing as well as could be expected of a ragged, washed-up fighter who'd taken the world's most famous dive.

The bus inched forward, but only enough to set the strap-hangers weaving slightly, then stopped dead again.

"You were good, you know," I said quietly. "You were really good, Vinnie. That time with Chico Perez. What was that? Three rounds? Hell, there was nothing left of him."

Vinnie nodded. "Nothing left," he repeated.

"And Harry Sermak. Two rounds, right?"

A nod.

The fact is, Irish Vinnie had never lost a single fight before Douggie Burns stroked his chin in the final round on that historic night at the Garden. But more than that, he had won decisively, almost always in a knockout, almost always before the tenth round, and usually with a single, devastating blow that reminded people of Marciano except that Vinnie had seemed to deliver an even more deadly killer punch. Like Brando, the better actor, once said, he "coulda been a contendah."

In fact he had been a contender, a very serious contender, which had always made his downfall even more mysterious to me. What could it have been worth? How much must Vinnie have been offered to take such a devastating dive? It was a riddle that only deepened the longer I pondered his current destitution. Whatever deal Spiro Melinas had made for Vinnie, whatever cash may have ended up in some obscure bank account, it hadn't lasted very long. Which brought me finally to the issue at hand.

"Too bad about. . . ." I hesitated just long enough to wonder about my safety, then stepped into the ring and touched my gloves to Vinnie's. "About . . . that last fight."

"Yeah," Vinnie said, then turned back toward the window as if it were the safe corner now, his head lolling back slightly as the bus staggered forward, wheezed, then ground to a halt again.

"The thing is, I never could figure it out," I added.

Which was a damn lie since you don't have to be a rocket scientist to come up with the elements that make up a fix. It's money or fear on the fighter's side, just money on the fixer's.

So it was a feint, my remark about not being able to figure out what happened when Douggie Burns's glove kissed Vinnie's cheek, and the Shameful Shamrock dropped to the mat like a dead horse, just a tactic I'd learned in business, that if you want to win the confidence of the incompetent, pretend to admire their competence. In Vinnie's case, it was a doubt I offered him, the idea that alone in the universe I was the one poor sap who wasn't quite sure why he'd taken the world's most famous dive.

But in this case it didn't work. Vinnie remained motionless, his eyes still trained on the window, following nothing of what went on beyond the glass, but clearly disinclined to have me take up any more of his precious time.

Which only revved the engine in me. "So, anybody else ever told you that?" I asked. "Having a doubt, I mean."

Vinnie's right shoulder lifted slightly, then fell again. Beyond that, nothing.

"The thing I could never figure is, what would have been worth it, you know? To you, I mean. Even, say, a hundred grand. Even that would have been chump change compared to where you were headed."

Vinnie shifted slightly, and the fingers of his right hand curled into a fist, a movement I registered with appropriate trepidation.

"And to lose that fight," I said. "Against Douggie Burns. He was over the hill already. Beaten to a pulp in that battle with Chester Link. To lose a fight with a real contender, that's one thing. But losing one to a beat-up old palooka like—"

Vinnie suddenly whirled around, his eyes flaring. "He was a stand-up guy, Douggie Burns."

"A stand-up guy?" I asked. "You knew Douggie?"

"I knew he was a stand-up guy."

"Oh yeah?" I said. "Meaning what?"

"That he was an honest guy," Vinnie said. "A stand-up guy, like I said."

"Sure, okay," I said. "But, excuse me, so what? He was a ghost. What, thirty-three, four? A dinosaur." I released a short laugh. "The last fight of his, for example. With Chester Link. Jesus, the whipping he took."

Something in Irish Vinnie's face drew taut. "Bad thing," he muttered.

"Slaughter of the Innocents, that's what it was," I said. "After the first round, I figured Burns would be on the mat within a minute of the second. You see it?"

Vinnie nodded.

"Then Douggie comes back and takes a trimming just as bad in the second," I went on, still working to engage Irish Vinnie, or maybe just relive the sweetness of my own vanished youth, the days when I'd huddled at the ringside press table, chain-smoking Camels, with the bill of my hat turned up and a press card winking out of the band, a guy right out of *Front Page*, though even now it seemed amazingly real to me, my newspaperman act far closer to my true self than any role I'd played since then.

"Then the bell rings on Round Three and Chester windmills Douggie all over again. Jesus, he was punch-drunk by the time the bell rang at the end of it." I grinned. "Headed for the wrong corner, remember? Ref had to grab him by the shoulders and turn the poor bleary bastard around."

"A stand-up guy," Vinnie repeated determinedly, though now only to himself.

"I was amazed the ref didn't stop it," I added. "People lost a bundle that night. Everybody was betting Douggie Burns wouldn't finish the fight. I had a sawbuck that he wouldn't see five."

Vinnie's eyes cut over to me. "Lotsa people lost money," he muttered. "Big people."

Big people, I thought, remembering that the biggest of them had been standing ringside that night. None other than Salmon Weiss, the guy who managed Chester Link. Weiss was the sort of fight promoter who wore a cashmere overcoat and a white silk scarf, always had a black Caddie idling outside the arena with a leggy blonde in the back seat. He had a nose that had been more dream than reality before an East Side surgeon took up the knife, and when he spoke, it was always at you.

Get the picture? Anyway, that was Salmon Weiss, and everybody in or around the fight game knew exactly who he was. His private betting habits were another story, however, and I was surprised that a guy like Irish Vinnie, a pug in no way connected to Weiss, had a clue as to where the aforementioned Salmon put his money.

"You weren't one of Weiss's boys, were you?" I asked, though I knew full well that Vinnie had always been managed by Old Man Melinas.

Vinnie shook his head.

"Spiro Melinas was your manager."

Vinnie nodded.

So what gives? I wondered, but figured it was none of my business, and so went on to other matters.

"Anyway," I said. "Chester tried his best to clean Douggie's clock, but the bastard went all the way through the tenth." I laughed again.

The bus groaned, shuddered in a blast of wind, then dragged forward again.

"Well, all I remember is what a shellacking Douggie took."

Vinnie chewed his lower lip. "'Cause he wouldn't go down."

"True enough. He did the count. All the way to the last bell."

Vinnie seemed almost to be ringside again at that long-ago match, watching as Douggie Burns, whipped and bloody, barely able to raise his head, took punch after punch, staggering backward, fully exposed, barely conscious, so that it seemed to be a statue Chester Link was battering with all his power, his gloves thudding against stomach, shoulder, face, all of it Douggie Burns, but Douggie Burns insensate, perceiving nothing, feeling nothing, Douggie Burns in stone.

"Stayed on his feet," Vinnie said now. "All the way."

"Yes, he did," I said, noting the strange admiration Vinnie still had for Douggie, though it seemed little more than one fighter's regard for another's capacity to take inhuman punishment. "But you have to say there wasn't much left of him after that fight," I added.

"No, not much."

"Which makes me wonder why you fought him at all," I said, returning to my real interest in the matter of Irish Vinnie Teague. "I mean, that was no real match. You and Douggie. After that beating he took from Chester Link, Douggie couldn't have whipped a Girl Scout."

"Nothing left of Douggie," Vinnie agreed.

"But you were in your prime," I told him. "No real match, like I said. And that . . . you know . . . to lose to him . . . that was nuts, whoever set that up."

Vinnie said nothing, but I could see his mind working.

"Spiro. What was his idea in that? Setting up a bout between you and Douggie Burns? It never made any sense to me. Nothing to be gained from it on either side. You had nothing to gain from beating Douggie . . . and what did Douggie have to gain from beating you if he couldn't do it without it being a . . . I mean, if it wasn't . . . real."

Vinnie shook his head. "Weiss set it up," he said. "Not Mr. Melinas."

"Oh, Salmon Weiss," I said. "So it was Weiss that put together the fight you had with Douggie?"

Vinnie nodded.

I pretended that the infamous stage play that had resulted from Weiss's deal had been little more than a tactical error on Vinnie's part and not the, shall we say, flawed thespian performance that had ended his career.

"Well, I sure hope Weiss made you a good offer for that fight, because no way could it have helped you in the rankings." I laughed. "Jesus, you could have duked it out with Sister Evangeline from Our Lady of the Lepers and come up more."

No smile broke the melancholy mask of Irish Vinnie Teague.

I shook my head at the mystery of things. "And a fix to boot," I added softly.

Vinnie's gaze cut over to me. "It wasn't no fix," he said. His eyes narrowed menacingly. "I didn't take no dive for Douggie Burns."

I saw it all again in the sudden flash of light, Douggie's glove float through the air, lightly graze the side of Vinnie's face, then glide away as the Shameful Shamrock crumpled to the mat. If that had not been a dive, then there'd never been one in the history of the ring.

But what can you say to a man who lies to your face, claims he lost the money or that it wasn't really sex?

I shrugged. "Hey, look, it was a long time ago, right?"

Vinnie's red-rimmed eyes peered at me intently. "I was never supposed to take a dive," he said.

"You weren't supposed to take a dive?" I asked, playing along now, hoping that the bus would get moving, ready to get off, be done with Vinnie Teague. "You weren't supposed to drop for Douggie Burns?"

Vinnie shook his head. "No. I was supposed to win that fight. It wasn't no fix."

"Not a fix?" I asked. "What was it then?"

He looked at me knowingly. "Weiss said I had to make Douggie Burns go down."

"You had to make Douggie go down?"

"Teach him a lesson. Him and the others."

"Others?"

"The ones Weiss managed," Vinnie said. "His other fighters. He wanted to teach them a lesson so they'd . . ."

"What?"

"Stay in line. Do what he told them."

"And you were supposed to administer that lesson by way of Douggie Burns?"

"That's right."

"What'd Weiss have against Douggie?"

"He had plenty," Vinnie said. "'Cause Douggie wouldn't do it. He was a stand-up guy, and he wouldn't do it."

"Wouldn't do what?"

"Drop for Chester Link," Vinnie answered. "Douggie was supposed to go down in five. But he wouldn't do it. So Weiss came up with this match. Between me and Douggie. Said I had to teach Douggie a lesson. Said if I didn't . . ." He glanced down at his hands. ". . . I wouldn't fight no more." He shrugged. "Anyway, I wasn't supposed to lose that fight with Douggie. I was supposed to win it. Win it good. Make Douggie go down hard." He hesitated a moment, every dark thing in him darkening a shade. "Permanent."

I felt a chill. "Permanent," I repeated.

"So Weiss's fighters could see what would happen to them if he told them to take a dive and they didn't."

"So it wasn't a fix," I said, getting it now. "That fight between you and Douggie. It was never a fix."

Vinnie shook his head.

The last words dropped from my mouth like a bloody mouthpiece. "It was a hit."

Vinnie nodded softly. "I couldn't do it, though," he said. "You don't kill a guy for doing the right thing."

I saw Douggie Burns's glove lift slowly, hang in the air, then drift forward, soft and easy, barely a punch at all, then Irish Vinnie Teague, the Shameful Shamrock, hit the mat like a sack of sand.

The hydraulic doors opened before I could get out another word.

"I get off here," Vinnie said as he labored to his feet.

I touched his arm, thinking of all the times I'd done less nobly, avoided the punishment, known the right thing to do, but lacked whatever Irish Vinnie had that made him do it, too.

"You're a stand-up guy, Vinnie," I said.

He smiled softly, then turned and scissored his way through the herd of strap-hangers until he reached the door. He never glanced back at me, but only continued down the short flight of stairs and out into the night, where he stood for a moment, upright in the elements. The bus slogged forward again, and I craned my neck for a final glimpse of Irish Vinnie Teague as it pulled away. He stood on the corner, drawing the tattered scarf more tightly around his throat. Then he turned and lumbered up the avenue toward the pink neon of Smith's Bar, a throng of snowflakes rushing toward him suddenly, bright and sparkling, fluttering all around, like a crowd of cheering angels in the dark, corrupted air.

THE LESSON
OF THE SEASON

It was the final minutes of the final day before Christmas, and Veronica Cross wanted only to pass these last moments sitting silently behind the register, her attention fixed on the book that rested in her lap. She had worked at the Mysterious Bookshop for almost ten years, but only on Saturdays, when the owner was at his house in Connecticut, and the store's full-time employees were scattered about various apartments throughout the city. Her job was simply to buzz customers into the store, answer whatever questions they asked, take their money, bag their purchases, then buzz them back out onto 56th Street. Almost no intellectual energy was required on Veronica's part, and the small financial supplement her salary added to her "real job" as a freelance copy editor made it possible for her to buy books from other stores, along with an occasional dinner out, or perhaps a discount ticket to a Broadway show.

The dinner and show might be enjoyed along or with one of her friends, someone like herself, who read good books and could articulately discuss them. As for romance, she'd more or less given up on that. Most men were little boys, needy and selfish, and none had ever struck her as worth the effort it took to dress up and preen and put on a happy face when she well knew that after the first few minutes she'd want only to hail a cab, return home, crawl into bed and open a book.

As for dress, she opted for modest elegance, long solid-colored skirts and dark-hued blouses for the most part, though black jeans with an accompanying black turtleneck sweater were not beyond her. Physically, she was tall, lithesome, and incontestably attractive, but for all that, she preferred to blend into whatever woodwork surrounded her. That other people chased distant stars, felt imperial urges, sought fame, or at least notoriety, all of that was a mystery to Veronica because she wished only to be left alone with her books.

She glanced at the clock at the rear of the room, then at her watch to verify the clock's correctness. Both sentenced her to fifteen more minutes of minding the store, and given the heavy snow that had begun to fall outside, she thought it quite likely that she might be able to pass those final moments lost in her book, the store silent all around her, with nothing but the soft tick, tick of the clock to remind her that she was part of an all too human world.

Then it happened.

Someone buzzed.

Veronica glanced toward the door, recognized the mild, faintly hang-dog face she saw behind the glass, then pressed the buzzer and let him in.

His name was Harry Bentham, and he came to the store every Saturday, though usually not during the final minutes of the day, and never during the final minutes of the final day before Christmas when a heavy snow was falling outside.

"Hi," Harry said quietly as he stepped into the shop.

"Hi," Veronica replied in a voice that was not without welcome, but which did nothing to encourage a more extended greeting.

Harry slapped the melting flakes of snow that had accumulated on the shoulders of his worn gray overcoat and stepped nearer to one of the shelves.

Veronica returned to her book, knowing exactly what she would see should she glance up again: Harry facing a shelf of paperback novels, his wiry gray hair blinking dully in the overhanging light, his rounded shoulders slumped, his posture no less slumped, so that he seemed perpetually to be collapsing, or if not that, then held up by invisible strings that were themselves stretched and frayed and in imminent danger of snapping.

But saddest of all, Veronica thought, was that Harry never bought a good book, and thus had yet to experience

THOMAS H. COOK

the actual thrill of literature, the way a fine passage could lift you high above the teeming world, give you focus and a sense of proportion, allow a small life to expand.

In the years of Saturdays Veronica had spent behind the register, she'd come to divide humanity into those who read good books and those who read bad ones. As for Harry, he topped the list of readers who seemed to have no sense of what a book was for, that it could pull you deeper into life, direct your concentration toward things that really mattered, give voice to longing, prepare you for death. At no time during the ten years of her stewardship had Harry ever bought a hardback book. In fact, he had rarely even risen to the level of literature that had at least been briefly housed between hard covers. No, Harry was not only a reader of bad books, he was a reader of paperback originals, a reader of work so entirely without merit, so utterly devoid of any enduring quality of style or story or idea, that even the work's publisher had opted to present it in a form doomed to vanish at the first approach of mold.

"Uh . . ." Harry said tentatively. "Veronica?"

Veronica looked up from her book.

"You don't have the new Bruno Klem, do you?"

Bruno Klem was the author of a decidedly lowbrow series of paperback originals known to its few aficionados as "The Crime Beat Chronicles." From the garish covers, the novels appeared to take place in a neon lit city of strip clubs and after hours bars in which he-man detective Franklin

Lord battled the dastardly minions of Oslo Sinestre, the series' arch villain.

"It hasn't come in yet," Veronica said. She offered a quick smile, then returned her attention to *The Measure of Man*, a book which was, according to the jacket copy, "a beautifully written and philosophically astute meditation on the moral complexity of human life as seen through the eyes of a defrocked Venezuelan priest."

She turned the page. "We live in the echo of our pain," she read silently.

She glanced up from the book and watched Harry's back, the way his right hand lifted tentatively toward a particular book, then drew away and sank into the pocket of his frayed coat. He was no doubt preparing to make a selection, and she found herself hoping that something would seize him suddenly, direct his attention to the neighboring shelf where he might find a work of actual merit, one that would enlarge his appreciation of what a book can do, how it can draw you down to previously unplumbed depths of understanding.

But Harry remained in place, and so Veronica returned her attention to the book.

We live in the echo of our pain.

She pondered the phrase and for some reason, impossible to fathom, found herself seated near her father's hospital bed, the old man stretched out on his back, tubes running here and there, an oxygen mask over his mouth and nose so that he looked like an astronaut carefully strapped in for the outward voyage.

He had died eight years before, when Veronica had been twenty-one years old, living in her Park Slope apartment—Manhattan being far too expensive—and eking out the same modest living in the same poorly paid trade she still practiced. She'd sat with him each night during the final days of his life, done what she'd thought required of an only child, the daughter of a divorced father who'd outlived not only her mother, but the two wives he'd later married and divorced, so that by the time of his final illness, there'd been no one who felt the slightest obligation toward him, save Veronica. He had been a wealthy real estate agent until suddenly, at the first onset of middle age, he'd gone completely nuts, sold the agency, and begun spending money hand over fist or losing vast quantities of it in cruelly expensive divorce settlements. Year by year his fortune had dwindled, until the last of it had vanished by the time Veronica had graduated from high school, selected an Ivy League college, applied, been accepted, then learned to her shock and dismay that her father had even squandered the money he had previously set aside for her education, spending every penny of it on high-roller gambling trips to Las Vegas, extravagant parties at the Pierre, wining and dining an army of fortune-seeking bimbos, and finally on a yacht he'd anchored briefly off Fire Island, then sold at a huge loss to an oil man from Houston. The yacht had been the old man's last costly asset, and he'd used the proceeds of its sale on such stylish perishables as watches and hand-tailored suits, all of which he had later palmed off to various

Second Avenue consignment shops, after which, with truly nothing left, he had sunk into absolute penury.

As a result, Veronica had been forced to waitress during the day and at night attend classes at Hunter College, from which she had finally graduated, but with a diploma that could not compete with the Ivy League educated and equally striking coeds who thronged about the great publishing houses of New York. Thus, she had been relegated to the decidedly unglamorous world of freelance editors, living from manuscript to manuscript, and thus from hand to mouth, a condition to which she had adapted quite well. In recent years, she had even concluded that hers was a superior position since she didn't have to kiss anyone's ass and could, with few exceptions, select the titles she wished to edit and avoid the utter trash that salaried employees could not.

We live in the echo of our pain.

She turned the phrase over in her mind, and wondered why it had returned her to her father's bedside during his bleak final days, the smelly hospital ward in which she'd sat night after night, and which she had only left after he'd released his last breath. It was miraculous, really, the way a few words could summon you back to past experiences, illuminate the shadowy corridors of that backward journey, allow it to resonate within you. Such was the true value of literature, she decided, that it gave life a resounding echo.

"You don't read Bruno Klem?"

Veronica glanced up to see Harry Bentham staring at her, his face barely visible behind the huge black plastic frame of his glasses.

"No, I don't."

Harry nodded slowly and turned back to the shelves, moving his face closer to the individual paperback spines, intently focused on each one, as far as Veronica could tell, as if he were searching for the answer to life among the volumes he found there.

But what answer could you possibly expect to find among the paperback originals, Veronica wondered. Where in any of those inferior volumes could pain's echo rise from the page and in that rising address the great mystery of how we came to be the one we are, how we should proceed, what we should seek in the brevity of our days, and what forgo? In a room filled with mysteries, this seemed the deepest of them all, one Veronica now determined to have answered at least as far as Harry Bentham could answer it.

She closed *The Measure of Man* and sat back, pressing her spine against the wall behind her. "I have a question," she said.

Harry turned, clearly surprised that she had addressed him.

"Why do you read Bruno Klem?"

Harry's thick, eerily purplish lips parted mutely.

"Every Saturday you come in here and buy five or six books," Veronica added. "Always Bruno Klem, or something like it. So, my question is, what do you get out of it? I'd really like to know."

Harry blinked slowly, removed his glasses, wiped them with a handkerchief drawn from his back pocket, and returned them to his face. "They're like a scotch to me," he said.

"A scotch?"

"You know, like when you come home at the end of a bad day, and maybe your wife is waiting for you, and she gives you a scotch."

Veronica knew that Harry Bentham had never been married, that no one waited for him with a drink in hand at the end of the day, but that was not the point.

"A book is a scotch?" she asked. "What does that mean?" She shook her head in exasperation. "Let me try a different direction. When did you start reading?"

"During the war," Harry said.

Judging by Harry's age, Veronica guessed that he meant the Vietnam War, but the precise military conflict to which he had referred was in no sense the issue. "When you were young then?" she asked.

"During the war," Harry repeated.

"Because you were bored?"

"No."

"Why then?"

Harry shrugged silently. He seemed reluctant to go on.

Veronica, however, was in no mood to take silence for an answer.

"Why then?" she repeated.

"We came in from a patrol," Harry answered. "Went to our tents. There was a book on one of the cots."

"What kind of book?"

"A little paperback," Harry said. He nodded toward the wall of paperback originals that rose behind him. "Bruno Klem." He shrugged again, his shoulders rising and falling ponderously. "The sergeant saw me moping around. He tossed me the book. 'Here,' he said, 'it'll take your mind off it.'"

"Off what?" Veronica asked.

"The patrol," Harry answered. "It was a bad patrol."

"Bad in what way?"

Harry drew in a long breath, one that trembled slightly. "We were all around this old man. Asking him questions. He was shaking his head no, he didn't know anything. We kept yelling and he kept shaking his head, you know?"

Veronica imagined the scene, Harry in his raw youth, small and bespectacled, his round shoulders slumped beneath the weight of whatever soldiers carry, canteens and ammo belts and some kind of rifle. He'd probably been the company geek, slow and ineffectual, a burden to the others. More than anything she imagined him naïve and innocent, a kid who'd stumbled into the army the way he might have stumbled into a job at the nearest shoe store and kept it for fifty years.

"It was really hot, and we'd lost some guys," Harry continued. "And the old man just kept shaking his head and saying he didn't know where the others were, the VC, I mean, the ones who'd killed, you know, some of us."

Now she saw him in a tight circle of other soldiers, all of them wet with sweat, covered in jungle debris, Harry the smallest, the least involved in the interrogation of the old man, wanting only to get away, find a little shade, take a listless snooze.

"Anyway, I started getting mad, you know?"

She could not imagine Harry Bentham mad any more than she could imagine him smart or passionate or good in bed. He was part of the great gray herd, a reader of trash, solitary, a flat-liner, J. Alfred Prufrock anesthetized upon a table.

"Mad?" she asked. "You?"

He seemed hardly to hear her, his eyes now distant but oddly charged, a strange, unsettling gleam replacing his usual dull stare.

"Something takes you," he said quietly. "It comes and it takes you."

She could feel a wave of heat coming from him, fierce and violent, as if from a raging furnace.

"Takes you," he repeated, almost to himself. "And you're gone."

He jerked his right hand from the pocket of his overcoat and formed it into a fleshy pistol, the index finger as its barrel.

"And so I yelled at him, and he kept saying no, and it was so hot, and I started yelling louder because we'd lost all these guys and so . . ." The index finger curled into a trigger finger and Harry's hand jerked. "So . . . I—" He stopped, thought for a moment, then added, "The other guys said it could happen to anybody. War and all. But it was murder. You can't deny it. It was murder, pure and simple."

He sank his hand deep into the pocket of his overcoat, and his voice lowered and its pace slowed to a melancholy crawl. "You think you're one thing, then suddenly, you're something else." He closed his eyes slowly, then opened them again. "Anyway, when I got back to camp, the sergeant tossed me this book and said it would take my mind off of it." A small, mournful smile played on his lips and his eyes glistened. "We all have things we want to forget, don't we?"

Suddenly, Veronica was with her father again, sitting in a chair, staring at him coldly, listening as his breath swept raggedly in and out until suddenly his eyes opened, and in a struggling tone, he called her name.

"Don't we?" Harry asked.

She saw herself rise and walk to the side of his bed, his eyes barely open, his lips moving frantically, repeating her name, *Veronica, Veronica.* She saw in his eyes a strangely desperate pleading, and felt that he was perhaps asking her forgiveness for the hardship to which his reckless self-indulgence had sentenced him. She started to answer him, soothe him, tell him that she loved him, that all was forgiven. But suddenly she considered the wasted fortune, the gray rooms of night school, her long days at a greasy diner, the cramped Brooklyn apartment, and a jolt of consuming anger shot through her, hot and jangling as a vicious electrical charge.

"Things that we did, that . . . you know . . ."

Now she was staring at the old man sullenly, coldly watching as his eyes closed and his lips parted breathlessly, her hand rising all the while, rising as if drawn into the air by a vast malignant power, furious, demented by rage, rising and rising, until it finally stopped, held an instant, then swept down in blistering fury, and in the echoing horror of the moment, she realized that she had slapped her dead father's face.

". . . things . . . we can't take back."

She drew in a shaky breath and all but shuddered in that remembered rage, all the fuming anger of her lost ambitions, her father's mad indifference, the blighted life that had been his, and which to some degree she had inherited, all of it in full, resounding echo, moving in seething waves over and within and through her.

"Yes," she said. "We do."

Harry nodded. "Anyway, the book worked," he said. "I been reading them ever since."

She thought of Harry now, the echoing violence in which he lived, how it must endlessly swell and eddy in dark and bloody currents, Bruno Klem the wall he raised against them, and behind which he labored to secure a simple, decent life. What had he been before that distant murder, she wondered. What life had he imagined for himself? Had he even remotely guessed that in that single pistol blast he would equally destroy a future wife and children, a life lived in something other than the moral bafflement that now held his heart in thrall, and from which he sought brief escape in the preposterous antics of paperback heroes who shot it out with unreal villains in worlds where the moral lines were never blurred.

She rose, walked over to the shelf behind Harry and drew out the first paperback installment of a new action series. Then she turned and handed him the book, softly, affectionately, as she thought a loving wife might hand him a scotch at the end of a long, bad day. "Try this," she said. "It's by a new author. There'll be lots of books in the series."

Harry took the book. "Thanks," he said, then paid her and left the store, his shoulders hunched against the outer chill, the falling snow.

Veronica returned to her place, retrieved *The Measure of Man* from where she'd placed it on top of the register, and opened it.

We live in the echo of our pain.

The line was still moving through her mind a few minutes later when she placed the book in her bag, turned out the lights, locked the door, and thus secured the merely literary mysteries behind an iron gate.

On the long subway ride to her small, book-stuffed studio in Park Slope, she sat silently, with her hands in her lap. Normally, she would have read her book during the ride home, keep her eyes fixed on the words, turning the pages without ever looking up. But now she took time to consider the other people on the train, wondering what dark, unspoken things might have befallen them, what sorrows they had suffered, witnessed, caused, the varied ways they'd managed to endure the life that followed. In all of that, we were the same, she decided, bent on finding comfort in whatever way we can.

Once she'd peered briefly at each face opposite her, she lifted her eyes to the lighted advertising panel that shone above them. It showed a Christmas tree on a busy corner, a man in uniform holding a red bucket, people dropping change into charity's deep well. She drew her gaze from the photograph, thought of Harry, then of herself, then of the others on the train, in the city, on the planet.

It was the lesson of the season, she supposed, that all of them . . . are you.

THE ODDS

The paired numbers shot through his mind in quick metallic bursts, the dry slap of bullets hitting beach sand. It is the way he'd lived, like a man under fire, raked by numbers, no trees to shield him, no foxholes, only the endless open beach, with no sun or moon above him, just the melancholy stare of her sea-blue eyes.

"Who is he, anyway?"

"Eddie Spellacy."

He heard his brother Jack's true voice for the first time in almost thirty years, heard it as it actually sounded, not over the phone, but here, beside his bed.

"Eddie the Odds, they called him."

There was a hopeless sorrow in Jack's voice, a yearning for things to have turned out differently, and so he didn't open his eyes because he knew that his brother's long sad face would break his heart.

"He was always figuring the odds."

"The odds on what?"

"Everything, I guess. But he made his living figuring them on horses."

The voices came from a world he could not live in, where men and women moved easily about, heedless of the way things really were, the awesome knowledge that was his, how the odds, no matter what they seemed, could abruptly change. Her sad sweet voice curled through his mind, *What's wrong, Eddie?* Even then, his answer, thrown over his shoulder as he fled from her, had seemed more truth than lie, *I just have to go.*

"They find him on the street?"

"No, he had a room. Nothing more than that. He didn't need anything more. He'd stopped seeing other people years ago. Even me. He said he'd figured the odds that on the way to his place something might happen to me. A car wreck. A plane crash. Too risky, he told me. Anything can happen."

"So how'd he get to the hospital?"

"He had a heart attack. Somebody heard him moaning in his room, I guess. Called 911. I don't know who called. Just someone."

Someone, but not her, Eddie thought. Someone anonymous, a neighbor down the hall who knew only that the guy in Room 603 was Eddie the Odds, one of nature's freaks, a human calculator who never went out, was never seen, never visited, with no dog, no cat, with nothing but his streaming numbers. Eddie the Odds. Eddie the Oddball.

He twisted about violently, the odds streaming through his head, each number an accusation, reminding him of that day, the sudden movement, the heavy fall, the way she'd seen him in the playground the next day, started toward him, the look in her eyes as he'd risen and walked away. He'd wanted to tell her what had happened, but what were the odds she'd have felt the same about him after that? What were the odds she'd ever laugh with him again, or touch his hand?

"So all these years he just stayed in his room and figured the odds?"

"Yeah."

"On what?"

"On crazy stuff. Whenever a tree would fall or a car would jump the curb. Stuff like that. He never got close to anyone. Never married, had kids. He was afraid the odds were against them if he did. That he increased the odds. He said he couldn't help it. It was something his mind couldn't stop doing. All day, figuring the odds."

"So he's like . . . deranged?"

Yes, Eddie thought. As deranged as someone who washes his hands a hundred times a day, repeats the same phrases over and over and over, turns off the light a thousand times or compulsively opens and reopens the refrigerator before he can withdraw that single bottle of hyper-filtered water. He'd finally turned it into a profession, the only choice he'd had since the fearful results of his compulsion had made it impossible for him to do anything else. He couldn't go to an office, couldn't have a profession.

"So when did this thing start, this thing with the odds?"

"When he was still a kid."

"What did it start with?"

"I don't know."

With a girl, Eddie answered now, though without speaking, keeping his secret safe, the odds now incalculably vast against his ever revealing it. Her sea-blue eyes rose like two lost moons over a turbulent river of rapidly streaming numbers.

She.

The only one he'd ever loved.

He saw her as she looked the morning she'd first come to Holy Cross, Margaret Shaunassey, twelve years old, a new girl in the neighborhood, with a smile like spring rain and sea-blue eyes. What were the odds, he'd asked himself at that first moment, that she would even notice him, a kid from West 47th Street, Eddie the kidder, Eddie the goof, a schoolyard prankster, tall for his thirteen years, with a freckled face he could do anything with, shape like dough, turn tragic or comic by turns, hide all his shyness and uncertainty behind.

"So he's been this way his whole life?"

"Not his whole life. But most of it. It came on him when he was thirteen."

Thirteen, Eddie thought as he lay silent and unmoving, save for the backward journey of his mind. Thirteen and in love with Margaret Shaunassey. But what were the odds that he could win her against the likes of handsome boys like Angelo Balderi and smart ones like Herbie Daws? Not very good, he guessed, but in that same instant he knew he would shirk off all his fearful lack of confidence, and boldly go where he had never gone, go there with everything on the line, all his chips on this one number, spin the wheel, regardless of the odds.

"And since then?"

"Since then, he's been Eddie the Odds."

Eddie the Odds, alone in a cramped little room in a Brooklyn hotel, staring at Manhattan, but never going there, because he couldn't stop his mind from figuring the odds of a subway accident or a bus collision or the even greater odds against a flooded tunnel or collapsing bridge, odds that were constantly changing, like the flipping numbers on that immense scheduling board he'd once seen in Grand Central, odds forever racing by at an impossible click, turning on him suddenly, throwing endless strings of calculations, odds that exploded all around him, hurling earth and shrapnel, lighting his inner sky with millions of sparks. But worst of all, as he knew too well, they were odds that he increased simply by being on that train or bus, increased by being the carrier of bad luck, misfortune like a virus he could spread to anyone, and so increased the odds that the little girl next to him on the subway or the little boy beside him on a bus would be dead, dead, dead. Dead because of him. Dead because he defied the odds, brought death with him where he stood and where he went, untimely death, against all odds.

He felt his fingers draw into a fist, then the fist thrust outward, the way it had that morning, just a little shove, but one that had finally recoiled and come rushing back toward him, invisibly penetrating the hard bone of his skull, reconfiguring his brain in a freakish and irrevocable way, turning him into what he had become since then, Oddball Eddie, Eddie the Odds.

In a quick vision, he saw the home he might have had, and had so often imagined during the long years he'd lived in his small cramped room. A large house with a large yard, kids playing on the green lawn, and she there too, the one he'd done it for, Margaret Shaunassey, the girl with the spring-rain smile.

He'd first spotted her in the school playground, and against the odds, approached her.

I'm Eddie Spellacy.

Hi.

You're new, right?

Yes.

After that it had been all jokes, and Eddie the jokester had made her laugh and laugh, laugh until her eyes watered and she fought for breath and clutched her sides and begged him to stop, stop, because it was killing her, this laughter.

And so he'd stopped, fallen silent, then, more in love than anyone in books or movies, revealed the mission of his lovesick heart.

I'll always look out for you.

And he'd meant it, too, meant it as deeply as he'd ever meant anything. He would be her knight, escort her through the mean streets of Hell's Kitchen, fend off the neighborhood dragons, its street toughs and bullies, protect her from catcalls and leering glances, and still later, as they grew older, married and had children, he would protect her from the fear of loss and abandonment, the dread of loneliness and the steady drip of age. He would do all of this. And he would do it forever. He would never cease, until she was safely home.

You can feel safe with me, Margaret.

That was when she'd reached into her lunch box and offered him one of her mother's homemade cookies.

I do feel safe with you, Eddie. I really do.

What else is there but this? he wondered now, the thought cutting through the flaming trails of exploding odds. What else is there for a boy but this offer of protection? If he had ever known nobility, it was then. If he had ever known courage or self-sacrifice, these had come to him through her, fallen cool and sweet upon his shoulders like spring rain. All he had ever wanted was joined with her, his hope for marriage, family, an ordinary life.

And against all odds he had lost it.

A new voice cut through the fireworks of numbers, returning him to the here and now.

"I'm Doctor Patel. Your brother looks agitated."

"Yes, he does."

"I could give him something to help him relax."

His endlessly churning brain immediately figured the odds against just slipping away, quietly and without fuss, a welcomed end to laying odds, and in that instant he tried to imagine the cooling of his brain, its inflamed circuitry finally soothed, the flood of numbers it sent like flaming stones through his mind now little more than a quiet mound of dying embers. If he could just get to the point of rest, that place where his mind could embrace the sleep for which he'd yearned since that day.

That day.

He saw it dawn over the city, a warm glow that slanted through his tenement window and curled around him and seemed almost to lift him from his bed and send him on his way, out onto the street and down the avenue to where the sweet and lovely Margaret Shaunassey waited for him each morning, her books in her arms before he drew them from her and together they set off for school. He had during those brief preceding weeks been one of life's winners, the boy who'd won the heart of the kind and beautiful Margaret Shaunassey, she of spring rain and sea-blue eyes. No more Eddie the prankster, with his gapped teeth. No more Eddie the loser, with his indifferent grades. Because of her, because of the love he'd won from her deserving heart, he'd become the walking Miracle of Holy Cross, looked at in wonder by the other boys, the guy who most among them had truly beaten the odds.

"Mr. Spellacy, you're going to feel a slight pinch."

He did, and with its bite he suddenly found himself lifted and carried away on a river of exquisite softness. The eternally cascading numbers slowed and after a time he became pure sensation, beyond the reach of clearly defined thoughts or expressions. Here, levitated, he had no need for devices of any kind, no need for pencils, or racing forms, or the little scraps of paper on which he figured the odds against this horse or that one winning this race or that one. The world of racetrack betting, of starting bells and photo finishes, now lay decidedly in the past, the odds against returning to it increasing with each passing second. He felt only the silent churn of his body drifting delicately forward, as if on a pillow of air, moving steadily and smoothly toward a final endless calm.

Only his thoughts were as weightless as he was. They came and went effortlessly, like small eddies within the gently flowing current. Translucent faces swam in and out as he lay silent and without fret, his bed now a raft gliding peacefully down a misty river. They stayed only a moment, these faces, then faded back into the mist. His mother, her hair pulled back, peering into a steaming kettle of corned beef and cabbage. His father's face, smudged with grease from the mechanic's shop. His older brother, Jack, all spit and polish in his army uniform.

The faces of horses surfaced, too, black or brown, with their huge sad eyes. They had given him more pleasure than any human being, and now, as he floated, they sometimes came rushing out of the engulfing cloud, strong and beautiful, their tails waving like banners in the bright summer air. Holiday Treat appeared, with Concert Master a link behind, noble in their ghostly strides, his only source of awe. They came prancing by the score, these horses upon which he had laid odds without dread. Something he'd never done with human games, baseball, football and the like, least of all on boxing. No, he had laid odds only on horses because though chance might rudely play upon them, it never fell with the dark intent of malicious force, and thus despite its storied wins and losses, for him the track remained unbloodied ground.

Suddenly, he saw a head slam into a brick wall, a splatter of blood left behind, and closed his already closed eyes more tightly, working to seal off this vision, return it to the darkness.

It worked, and in the blackness, he felt the raft move on, bearing him gently away, down the placid, mist-covered stream. As he drifted, he saw a few friends from his boyhood, but none beyond those early years because his mind's obsessive calculations had figured the odds against having friends his evil, odds-defying presence would not harm. He'd done the same with marriage and parenthood, and so no wife or child greeted him from the enfolding mist. The odds, as his eternally fevered brain had so starkly calculated, were against the safe passage of anyone who walked beside him or even passed his way.

A newspaper headline abruptly streamed through his mind, the words carried on a lighted circle, like the zipper on Times Square: LOCAL BOY DIES IN FREAK ACCIDENT.

Freak accident.

It had begun the morning after he'd first heard the news that a local boy had tripped and fallen, slammed his head against a nearby wall, and by freak accident, died as a result. He'd stepped out of his third-floor apartment, on his way to school, when he'd glanced down the flight of stairs that led to the street. What were the chances, his mind had insistently demanded, of someone falling down them, *because they were with him*? He'd frozen in place, with his hand on the banister, briefly unable to move before he'd finally regained some control over his mind's building oddity, then walked slowly, with a disturbing caution, down the uncarpeted steps.

She'd been waiting for him at the corner, just as she'd waited for him every morning for the last few weeks, her eyes upon him with unimaginably high regard, never noticing his hand-me-down clothes, the gap between his teeth, seeing what no other girl had ever seen, the nobility he craved, tender and eternal, his ragged knighthood. But now she seemed to stand amid a whirl of wildly hurtling traffic, a universe of randomly flying objects, the cement curb no more than a trapdoor over a terrible abyss, a door held in place only because he did not join her there, he, Eddie, against whom the odds were cruelly pitted, Eddie who brought misfortune, imperiling by his own ill luck everyone he loved.

And so he'd turned from her, and walked away, turned from her sea-blue eyes and spring-rain smile, and glimpsed, in his turning, a dimming of those eyes, a winter in the rain.

"I think my brother needs more."

"It's dangerous, Mr. Spellacy."

"How long does he have anyway?"

"Not long."

"Then it doesn't matter. He just wants to rest."

Another pinch and the voices ceased and night fell abruptly within his mind, sweeping everything from view. For a long time he lay, breathing softly in the mahogany blackness. Then from the depths of that impenetrable darkness, he sensed movement, but saw nothing, no relatives, no horses. Seconds passed. Or minutes. Or days. And far, far away, a tiny light emerged, pinpoint small at first, but growing like the dawn, until once against he was on the pillow of silence, drifting down a watery corridor of hazy light.

Still alive, he thought disconsolately, though this knowledge did not come to him as words spoken silently by his mind, but as a sensation mysteriously carried on the subtle beat of his pulse. It was like all his thinking now, composed not of coherent thoughts, but rather the product of unpredictable mental surges, the firings of his brain tapping out codes that seemed to be transmitted, soundlessly and without grammar and syntax, to his decoding heart.

Freak accident.

Night fell within him again, but not the blackness he sought, the dead calm of oblivion. Instead, it was the mottled darkness of his spare room. Within that room, he saw nothing but the gray-and-white flickering of the small television he kept on the tiny card table where he dined each night on food that required no cooking, since he'd figured the odds that a single match, used to light the single eye of a small gas range, might set his room on fire, then the hotel, then the neighborhood, a whole city ignited because Eddie the Odds defied the odds, Eddie, whose cautiously discarded match, dipped in water, cold to touch, might yet devour millions in whirling storms of flame.

A horn blared in his mind, and the flickering screen dissolved into a view of the track, the horses prancing toward the starting gate, Light Bender in sixth place, hustled unwillingly into her stall, the odds against her ten-to-one.

Now a pistol shot rang out, and they were off, Light Bender in tenth place as he'd figured she would be, but moving in ways he'd failed to calculate, her head thrust forward like a battering ram, her stride lengthening, as it seemed, with each forward thrust, her black mane flying as she tore down the track, black hooves chewing up the turf.

From his gently flowing pallet of air, he watched as she rounded the track, eighth, seventh, sixth, now moving within striking distance of a fabled win. Then, suddenly, she began to fall apart, fall into pieces, like a shattered puzzle, her hooves no longer connected to her legs, her haunches no longer connected to her torso, her head thrust out farther than her long neck as if it were trying to outrun the rest of her.

He felt a violent agitation in his drift, and behind closed eyes looked to his right, if it were his right, and there was Light Bender running at full speed beside him, racing the fiercely boiling current, but running without legs, and now without a body, and finally without a head, so that nothing was left but her mane, long and black and shimmering . . . like Margaret Shaunassey's hair.

Without warning she appeared before him as she had so many, many times, come like an incubus to pry open the still unmended rift within him, the cut that bled a crimson stream of numbers, and from which spilled, on each red molecule, the odds against his life.

She stood in front of Holy Cross School on West 43rd Street. He wasn't sure he'd ever actually seen her on the steps of the school, though even if he had, she'd have been standing under the red-brick entrance marked GIRLS, not as she was now, poised between that entrance and the BOYS on the opposite side of the building. She stood silently, with her arms at her sides, dressed in her school uniform of white blouse, checkered skirt, white socks, black shoes. Margaret Shaunassey. How kind she would have been, a wordless impulse told him, to horses.

He felt the flow increase in velocity, make a hard left-ward turn, then descend, so that he felt himself sliding down a long metal chute. As he slid, he sensed the air grow warm around him. A cloud of steam drifted up and blurred his vision of Margaret but not his memory of her, which became all the more vivid as the steam thickened around him. It was as if his experience of her had become even more sharply defined, everything else a blur, the difference, as he conceived it, between a great horse recalled in the moment of its triumph and one recalled as merely another head nodding from the starting gate.

He closed his eyes more tightly and tried to remain in the soothing comfort of darkness, settle back into the flow, move toward death without further delay or interruption. But the lighted string of numbers began to move again, a snake uncoiling in his head, bringing back the odds he'd obsessively figured during all the passing years, the vast eliminations they had cruelly demanded, hopes and plea-sures cut from him like strips of skin, all the sensual joys of life, taste and touch, the fierce reprieve of love, odds that had directed his life not according to the rules of probability but to the probability of error within those rules, the terrible intrusion of odds-defying chance.

Freak accident.

The speed of the current increased again, and he felt himself racing headlong into an area of shade, the vault of heaven, or wherever he was, turning smoky. Through the smoke, he saw a figure close in upon him, slowly at first, then astonishingly fast, as if he'd traveled the distance between them at warp speed, so that he instantly stood before him, silent in the smoldering air, a kid from Holy Cross, short with pumpkin-colored hair, a rosy-cheeked boy half his size, but the same age.

Mickey Deaver.

Mickey the Clown.

He felt his closed eyes clench, but to no avail, because the vision was inside him, carried toward him on a river of rushing numbers. It faded in and out, hazy at first, but with growing clarity, until at last the mist lifted and Mickey stood in his school uniform, twelve years old, holding a blood-spattered towel against the side of his head. He stared straight ahead. His eyes didn't blink. Not one red hair stirred. The only motion came from his lips, mouthing two unmistakable words:

Freak accident.

Now he was in the schoolyard, watching from a distance as Mickey sauntered over to Margaret. Within seconds she was laughing. Not very much at first, then harder and harder, as Mickey clowned and made jokes. Her laughter rang through the overhanging trees and spiraled around the monkey bars and curled through the storm fence against which he leaned, watching as Margaret reached into her small lunch box and handed Mickey the Clown one of her mother's cookies.

A siren split the air, and on its desperate keening, he felt a hard jolt in the flow, like a train going off the track, so that he gripped for a hold, now clinging for dear life as he bumped and clattered, the flow rocketing forward at what seemed inhuman speed. The river vanished and he was on land, his body flat on the hard surface of a metal gurney, wildly jostled as if he were being dragged across rutted ground.

"What's the matter, Doctor?"

"Quick, get the defibrillator!"

The explosion came from the center of his chest, as if he'd lain face down on a land mine. It blasted shards of light in all directions, flashing images of past time through a roiling stream of memory. He saw Mickey emerge, whistling happily, from the rear door of his building, then felt the brutal shove of his hand against Mickey's shoulder, and watched as Mickey tumbled to the side, knees buckling, so that his head struck hard against the side of the building, a geyser of blood spouting from his ear as he fell unconscious onto the cement stairs.

"Give me the paddles!"

A bell tolled, and in its dying echoes he saw Mickey gathered up, placed on a stretcher and wheeled into a waiting ambulance, a local boy, as the paper had described him, dead by freak accident.

"Clear!"

"Okay."

"Hit it!"

He felt the jerk of the gurney like blows to his body, wrenchingly painful punches that sent him into aching spasms each time another jolt rocked the earthbound flow. With each blow a bell tolled and a year passed and logged within those passing years he saw the outcome of his act, Old Man Deaver dead of drink, Margaret confused and shaken, never knowing why he'd turned from her that morning, nor even approached her again, never knowing that he was still Eddie, her white knight, bent on her protection, and so protecting her from himself, because by his own ill luck, a rift in the laws of chance, a little, half-hearted shove had made him a murderer.

"Clear!"

"Hit it!"

He jerked in pain, and through the screen of his pain yearned for the cushion of air, the invisible river, as his defiant brain worked feverishly to figure the odds that he might at least die beyond the reach of odds.

"No good."

But figure as he did, calculate and recalculate, the odds remained the same as long ago, when he'd first begun to lay them, high against stopping yourself in time, getting another chance, high as the odds, he finally concluded, against a peaceful death.

"Too late."

At least a billion to one, he figured on the dying breath of a final calculation.

But for the first time in a long time, he had figured them too low.

THE SUNGAZER

I met Marilyn when I was a sophomore in college. She came from a rural area of Indiana and had one of those prairie faces, all openness and unwrinkled space. Her forehead was so pale and smooth you could almost see the pattern of the clouds overhead. She wore country clothes, little cotton dresses ornamented by spiraling vines of red rosebuds or plain, solid-color skirt and sweater combinations which blended perfectly with the old fashioned brick and mortar buildings of the state university.

The year was 1968, that impractical time when the universities rose up in dreamy fervor for causes which seem as distant and unrealizable now as the crystal seas of Xanadu. Almost no one seemed to be pursuing a recognizable future.

Everyone was in the process of abandoning the established paths. Engineers were becoming English majors and fervently arguing about the proletarian novel. Lawyers were talking about neighborhood legal clinics and reinterpretations of the Constitution which would make possible a peaceful transition to paradise.

Marilyn seemed to walk through these dense proceedings incorporeally. She was shy in the presence of strangers and kept silent during the hottest debates. In class she rarely asked questions; and at the frenzied political rallies which seemed to spring up everywhere in those days, she maintained the stolid dignity of a statue amid a frivolous shower of confetti.

I was an advertising major. I had a way with words and saw a great future for myself in jingles. Most of my fellow students regarded me as a grinning mastodon, worth about as much to the coming liberation as a time/motion analyst. I responded to their windy idealism with a haughtiness of my own. While they played their mystical political games, I worked at getting ahead. While they hunkered over schemes for the Coming Order, I prepared for graduation, recognizing as I did that this tumult would soon lift, leaving their breezy illusions as dead and grounded as a pile of starched bones.

At first, I sensed Marilyn looked upon all of this with the same disdain. Her silence suggested superiority, and I began to look for her at those rallies I regularly attended for my own amusement. She was always there, always silent, her arms cradling textbooks, a rare sight in those days. Self-confident though I was, I was a little put off by Marilyn, a little daunted by her upright posture and terrible wholesomeness—a manifestation, I suspected, of impregnable virginity.

But eventually, her allure overcame my reservations, and I shifted among the chaotic crowds, edging closer and closer to her at each noisy protest. I ended up shoulder-to-shoulder with her by early fall, and during a lull in the "Dump the Hump" chanting, I made my move. "Much ado about nothing," I muttered.

Marilyn stared straight ahead.

"This stuff won't end the war," I said, this time loud enough so there could be no mistake as to whom I was speaking or what was being said.

"What will then?"

"I don't know."

"Excuse me," she said, elbowing her way into the crowd away from me.

——◦——

The next time I saw Marilyn she was crying. Sitting under a large tree in a remote part of the campus, her face tucked into a white lace handkerchief, she looked like a figure out of Robert Browning; the weeping maiden bereft of love. I could reduce anything to a cliché; in those days it seemed like the only intelligent thing to do.

"You okay?" I asked.

"Yes. Fine."

"It doesn't look like it."

"I just start crying sometimes. Over things in general."

"Things in general."

"Yes."

This didn't seem worth pursuing. "I spoke to you once at a demonstration."

"You did?"

"I said all this protest stuff didn't make any difference. You didn't like that very much. You walked away."

"I'm sorry."

"I got over it."

She nodded and began folding her handkerchief.

"Well, at least you're not crying now," I said. Even then it sounded like Ronald Colman comforting Greer Garson.

"It never lasts long," Marilyn said. "But it never really goes away either."

I had no idea what this "it" was, but I presumed it was something her mind had vastly overrated, the high-school sweetheart with the terminal disease, the brilliant pianist with his scorched, stubby fingers; I had heard it all.

"Well, maybe something to eat would ward it off."

We spent the next few hours hunched over a Formica table in the campus diner. She ate just as I had expected, delicately slicing her potatoes into tiny slivers, munching cautiously at the edges of her hamburger, eating as only certain women can, without seeming to move their mouths.

"What's your major?" she asked.

"Advertising. I'm good at ideas."

She nodded half-heartedly. It was one of those infuriating Sixties gestures, an accusation as well as an expression of disappointment, the sad, knowing priest before the intransigent heathen. "Don't be so damned arrogant," I said.

"Was I arrogant?"

"Yes, you always are. You social-activist intellectuals with your great schemes for the future."

"That's not true," Marilyn said.

"You make ordinary people feel like garbage."

"I don't mean to do that."

I let it pass. "Why were you crying this afternoon?"

"I don't know," she said.

At that moment, she seemed the most exotic creature on earth. It wasn't chemistry which brought Marilyn and me together; it was alchemy.

───◇───

Marilyn and I were married two years later in a civil ceremony. I had done well academically and landed a job at a prestigious Chicago advertising agency. It took Marilyn longer to find work, and the job she found didn't interest her very much. This intensified that dreamy quality in her which I had mistaken for insightful detachment in our college days. She used all the outmoded clichés to describe her situation. Jobs weren't "meaningful." She wanted to make a "contribution." But it seemed to me that behind all the rhetorical language there was some larger, incomprehensible goal toward which she could move only like a great lumbering bird. "The war is over," I said once at dinner. "That's what's bothering you."

Marilyn stared at her food.

"Well, I thought you'd all be happy now."

"Don't be ridiculous," Marilyn said.

I laughed. "Jerry Rubin's happy. He's selling self-help insurance. What does he call it, I wonder. Radical Positive Thinking?"

"Just be quiet, David."

"And Rennie Davis has found a leader he can trust. What is he, twelve years old?"

Marilyn got up to leave. I grabbed her hand. "Let's have a baby."

"No."

"Why not? People do, people our age. Isn't that a contribution?"

Marilyn pulled her hand free. "No."

Lisa was born a year and a half later, and Marilyn seemed to open up to her. I thought I must have been right, that this was it—a baby—what she needed to fill that void floating in her like a large cold bubble. For a while, Marilyn's unreachable discontent dissipated, and it looked

as though she was going to be fine, was going to accept
what even I knew now to be the limited nature of our life,
with its passionless necessities. I hoped she would accept
the rudimentary forms of contentment which were acces-
sible to us, the little triumphs of the office, the consolation
of the hearth. But there is a terrible routine to infancy,
not much room for imagination, and Marilyn finally drew
away from motherhood as a vocation.

But she did not draw away from Lisa, our daughter, and
during the next few years, she won her over completely,
won her over inadvertently and without connivance. For
there was something in Marilyn's remote yearning which
captured Lisa and held her. They spent hours and hours
together, Lisa listening intently while Marilyn told her
stories she had made up the night before—wild, improbable
stories of soaring and undisciplined beauty, stories which
leaped over the traditional boundaries of time and space
and logic like a whirlwind leaps a ditch, leaving all behind
it in awe and disarray.

During our last year in Chicago, Marilyn began
writing her stories down. I would come home and hear
her portable typewriter clattering in the little room she
had made into a study. Several times I could hear her humming along with the typewriter, as if orchestrating some
particular scene. The tone was sometimes light, sometimes
funereal, but it always held a certain air which was clear
and unmistakable, the sense of hindered ardor breaking
free. Several times I asked Marilyn what she was doing,

trying to show some interest. She said she was writing letters and left it at that.

—◇—

By the time I was transferred to New York, Marilyn and I paced the house like confused duelists, looking for our marks but afraid to turn, afraid to fire. I hoped the move would help us, and the day we arrived at our new house in New Jersey seemed to offer promise. It had the taste of newness in it, fresh and sweet as the breath of nursing babies.

We spent the next two days getting the rooms arranged, all the hundreds of little objects put in their proper places, a nook or drawer or shelf for every accretion of middle-class life. Marilyn did it with mechanical efficiency, hardly wasting a motion.

I was exhausted by the time we finished, late at night on the second day. We put Lisa to bed and sat down together on the sofa in the living room. "I guess your parents will want to visit us soon," I said. Both my parents had been killed in an automobile accident when I was six years old.

"Probably," Marilyn said.

I casually put my arm around her shoulder. "You did a good job getting everything organized."

"I want Lisa to have a room of her own."

"All right."

"Not a bedroom of her own, a work room."

"Okay," I said. I looked around. "Your parents will like this place."

"They should," Marilyn said. "It's just like theirs."

I felt a terrible wave of anger for Marilyn. I felt like hitting her, like slapping her face. Useless. Hitting Marilyn would have been like hitting a locked door, painful only to the damaged hand.

Instead, I got up and rushed to the kitchen, leaving her alone in the living room. I stayed there for almost half an hour, drinking one cup of coffee after another, expecting, hoping she would come in and sit down beside me so we could begin some blind but determined process of reconstruction or rejuvenation. She never did, and when I went back into the living room, it was empty.

She had gone to bed. She lay there rigidly, curled up under a stone-gray blanket. I doubted she was asleep, but it would not have mattered. Looking at the hard wall of her back in the lamplight at her left, it seemed to me our happiness—coming as it did in brief, chaotic spurts—was at best a weak, disgruntled army against the fortress of our need.

The next Monday I went to my job in Manhattan. I was introduced to everyone I would be working with. They were all very friendly and helpful. Several of them invited me to lunch, but I wanted to be alone, to try to think things through once again.

At noon I walked out of the office building and headed down 41st Street to Bryant Park behind the New York

Public Library. It was filled with people walking quietly along or knotted together listening to speakers and street musicians. Everything imaginable was being hawked. People were selling Atlantis and reincarnation and numerology. A group of Eastern cultists bobbed up and down in pink robes. There were miracle cures for the body and the mind. It was a festival of false redemptions and uncertain paths out of the mystery. The air was heavy with thwarted flight, and I felt my own sadness at Marilyn's poisonous discontent gathering round me like a vapor.

"You're full of crap," someone said.

I thought he must mean me, but it was directed at a large man dressed in a long blue robe who stood quietly within a circle of people. The man in the robe smiled with professional indulgence. "Anything is possible, my friend," he said.

"What do you mean anything?" someone asked.

I moved nearer to listen.

"The soul of man can fly to any heights," said the man in the robe. He had long black hair streaked with gray, and his beard was so massive it darkened his face like a shadow. "We are beyond limits but not beyond possibilities."

The crowd chuckled softly, but the man in the robe went on. "Everything we have attained was first of all a dream. I teach that we should dream and keep on dreaming."

"Maybe you should take time out to get a job," someone shouted, and the crowd laughed.

"Anything is possible," shouted the man in the robe.

"What can you do then," someone taunted, "perform miracles?"

"Anything is possible. As long as there is a will to do it."

"You're full of crap," someone said again, and with that the crowd began slowly to disperse.

The man in the robe watched them for a moment, then he said in a voice loud enough to bring them back, "I can do a thing you have never seen. I can do it with my will alone."

But the crowd continued to move away heedlessly.

"I can gaze on the sun!" shouted the man. "I can do it with my naked eyes! I can walk away unharmed!"

A few people turned toward him, and one of them said, "With shades, buddy?"

"With my naked eyes." He pointed to a shining square of sunlight. "Follow me," he said.

The crowd seemed to hesitate for a moment, seemed to calculate whether this man was worth a few more minutes.

"Come on now if you want to see something," shouted the man. He stood in the center of a large patch of light. He lifted his arm and pointed at the sun. "There it is. You want to see something, don't you? Well, now's your chance."

Haltingly, the crowd began to move toward the block of sun and the man standing in the center of it, his arms held tightly against his sides, his robe bleaching in the light.

When they had gathered around, an attentive audience once again, the man in the robe took several deep, athletic breaths and closed his eyes. "When I open my eyes again," he said solemnly, "they will be staring straight into the sun."

He hesitated a moment, took what seemed to be a brief, dramatic pause, then he opened his eyes.

The crowd seemed to draw in its collective breath.

He stood rigidly with his head tilted upward, his eyes staring wide open toward the sun, his eyebrows arched high up his forehead, holding his eyelids sternly open, exposing the entire balls of his eyes to the boiling light overhead. He did not blink as the tears began to bead instantly in the corners of his eyes.

"Stop it," someone whispered.

The staring eyes seemed transfixed. They began to pour forth a stream of tears, sweeping down from the withering sockets, down the cheeks and off the face, darkening the collar of his robe with tiny spots of moisture.

"Someone get a cop."

He continued to glare fiercely at the sun. His head became a mop of wet, tangled hair, but the eyes remained fixed as if they had left his body and had assumed an indomitable identity of their own and a will to victory over the sun itself—a triumph which was not his triumph but their triumph, the triumph of the eyes.

"Stop it, mister," said someone in a frightened voice. "This is going too far."

But still the eyes stared straight ahead with a terrible density of intent, still pouring out futile tears, still holding to the very center of the sun with the physical, tangible grasp of clawing hands.

The city seemed to stop its clang and hiss and whistle. It was only the eyes now in battle with the sun; only the dream of conquest and transcendence over the iron laws of light and flesh.

Someone tried to cover the eyes with his hands, but the man in the robe slapped them away ferociously and continued to stare at the sun, the eyes shining so terribly in the light that they seemed to cast of little orbs of flame.

After that, no one spoke. They stood silently and waited for the man in the robe to end it. Finally, he did, closing his eyes very slowly, very gracefully, with a poet's sullen grandeur.

A little patter of applause began among the people around him, but the man didn't wait to hear it. He bolted away quickly, moving almost at a trot toward 41st Street.

I followed him at a distance. On 41st Street he turned left out of the park and then left again into an alley near the library. I kept after him, not really knowing why but sensing that surge of the miraculous which crowds seem to feel in the wake of prophets.

The alley was a dead end, entirely empty except for a large metal drum resting next to a wall. I took a few steps and stopped.

I walked almost stealthily toward the drum, feeling like an intruder in the temple, expecting the man in the robe to leap out from behind the drum at any moment and shrivel me with embarrassment. But I kept going, and after a moment, I could hear a low moaning coming from behind the drum just beyond my vision. I nearly turned back at that, and I had to step forward quickly to keep from doing it.

At first he didn't see me. He was pressed firmly against the wall behind the drum, his legs pulled tightly together in a crouch, his knees directly under his chin. He was frantically applying a thick white cream to his eyes, rubbing it in with his fists and whimpering pathetically as he rocked back and forth on the balls of his feet. His eyes were covered with the cream; it oozed between his fingers like pasty globs of fat and plopped stickily onto his immaculate blue robe.

When he finally opened his eyes and saw me, it was obvious he recognized me instantly as one of the people who had witnessed his sungazing performance. I almost expected him to jump up and run away in a seizure of humiliation. But he didn't. He looked at me closely, silently, his lips parted only slightly in what looked to be an apology. It was the face that mattered. A look of deep, in-dwelling agony passed over it. It was the terrible pain of a man who cannot live without miracles in a world where there aren't any.

When I got home that night, I found a note from Marilyn saying she had left me. She had taken Lisa, of course, and she was very apologetic about that, admitting it wasn't fair. She had wanted to let me say goodbye to her, but she had felt there was no way other than to leave immediately, while the impulse was strong. Otherwise, she said, it would just keep going on, and she would never leave at all.

I wandered about the house for several hours after finding the note. I couldn't think what else to do. For a while all I could do was rage, but that was useless.

I ended up sitting in the kitchen the way I had the night before, drinking endless cups of coffee, trying to come to terms with what had happened. I saw Marilyn the night of our first date and gloated at what a helpless thing she had seemed to be. Then I remembered her stories, the way they turned upward, always at the end, toward some unreachable hope, and I cried remembering good times, bad times, never really sure where the good blended invisibly into the indifferent, then into the bad.

Around nine the phone rang. It was Marilyn.

"You found my note?"

"Yes," I said stiffly. "Where are you?"

"Pennsylvania. Some little town. I don't know for sure. We're going to Indiana for a while."

"Your parents?"

"Yes. I don't know where after that."

"Is Lisa all right?" I asked.

"Yes," Marilyn said. "I told her I had to get away. I told her other things will have to be settled later. There are lots of things we have to settle before . . ."

"We'll settle everything later, Marilyn."

"All right."

"Are you driving straight through? I mean to Indiana?"

"No, we'll stop at some motel tonight. Get up early in the morning, about dawn. Go the rest of the way tomorrow."

"Okay."

"Well, I'd better go."

"All right."

"I'll call you when we get home."

"Please do that, Marilyn. I just want to know you made it. You know, that you're safe."

"As soon as we get there, I'll call."

"Okay."

She hung up, leaving me standing absurdly, the dull buzz of the phone humming in my ear. I slammed the phone down, hoping she might somehow hear my rage and fearfully, repentantly, come back to me.

There was nothing to do the next morning but go to work. I had watched television until almost dawn, finally lapsing into nervous, tumbling sleep. I could not bear the idea of remaining in the house, in the suburbs, listening to the children in the street.

I set about making an ordinary day of it. I shaved and showered and dressed myself, trying as best I could to keep chin up, upper lip stiff, my eye, as they say, on the buttered side of life.

On the train into the city, I tried to interest myself in a newsmagazine, but the anger kept welling up in me, the feeling of unwarranted betrayal. What did she want, this woman I had been fool enough to marry? What would she do in Indiana, for God's sake? What would she do anywhere at all, except poison life with her discontent? Watching the murky towns of New Jersey pass by the window, I felt like something primed for explosion. If Marilyn had been within my grasp, I think I might have strangled her to death. I saw her as a little red ball of inchoate sensibilities, then as a tiny ravenous mouth gnawing insatiably at the lineaments of decent, ordinary life. The very image of her face in my mind sickened me almost physically.

At the office, I put all my will to the service of a calm, unruffled demeanor. I took my morning coffee and sipped it casually while staring sightlessly at the papers spread out across my desk, white and flat, a plain commercial snow.

After a while, Joe Thompson peeped into my office. "Hear the news?" he asked jubilantly.

"What news?"

"The Jefferson Recording Company ad won a prize," Joe said. He stepped into my office and clapped his hands happily. "Isn't that great?"

I nodded. "Yeah."

"We're having a celebration down in Harvey Field's office. Why don't you come on down."

I walked down to Harvey's office. It was crowded with ad men whooping and laughing and slapping each other on the back. Someone threw a shower of confetti into the air, and I saw Marilyn standing quietly in those other campus showers long ago, showers of words, dreams, hopes which had invigorated her, them, everyone, it seemed now, but me. And I also saw myself, not as I am but as I must have seemed to Marilyn: a man, like those around me, celebrating in a small, grim office; a man who was not only satisfied with the small victories but who never looked beyond them; a man who not only accepted ordinary life but sanctified it; a man who never meditated upon a stormy sky or cast his eye—however briefly—toward some distant, shining sun.

I walked to the window and looked out. The great buildings towered above me—silent, immobile, uninstructive. The sun cast deep gray shadows across the streets. It was this same sun which would light Marilyn's way. Standing where I was—dreaming of where she was—my soul suddenly pronounced a wild, cheering blessing on her head. I could see her clearly now, moving into the white, beaming heart of the country, moving sunward.

WHAT EDDIE SAW

"You know why you're here, Eddie?"

Eddie nodded. He knew that he'd been summoned to the police station because Sheila Longstreet had been missing for more than twenty-four hours. He was a friend of Sheila's, but Eddie saw that the detective knew more about him than that, knew more about him than he'd likely have known about any high school junior who made decent grades and never caused trouble. Clearly the detective knew what everybody else on Cape Cod knew, that Eddie Panacci was the Coed Killer's son.

"A couple of kids at school said that they saw the two of you together just before Sheila disappeared," the detective said.

Eddie saw that the kids had actually seen not just him and Sheila, but the Old Man, too. It didn't matter that he'd been murdered in a prison bathroom twelve years before, because his memory still haunted the woods of Cape Cod, lingered among its wavy dunes and misty bogs, swam in and out of the ghostly afternoon light when couples walked on lonely wooded trails. But more than anything, as Eddie saw, the Old Man lingered in Eddie himself. "You look like him," someone had once said, and each time Eddie glimpsed himself in a mirror, he saw the Old Man's full lips and dark sunken eyes.

"These kids said they saw you and Sheila at the general store. Around five yesterday afternoon. Nobody's seen Sheila since then."

Eddie saw that he was supposed to respond to this, but how could he? He'd seen Sheila get out of his car, walk away, look back, smile. He had no idea why she hadn't made it to her house only a short distance down Breakwater Road, but he knew that the detective wouldn't believe this. He sat at the little square table in a plaid shirt and faded jeans, but he knew that the detective saw him in the gray flannel work clothes, oily and bloodstained, that his father had buried, along with the bodies of the two women he'd strangled, in the gravelly soil of Nickerson State Park.

"How did you and Sheila happen to end up at the general store?"

"I don't know. We just sort of . . . ended up there."

"The two of you just sat in the car? Your car? The one you have out in the parking lot?"

"Yes."

"Would you mind if we took a look at your car, Eddie?"

"No, I wouldn't mind."

The detective exited the room, then returned to it. "Okay," he said. "Tell me about Sheila. What you two did yesterday afternoon."

Eddie saw Sheila's head loll to the right, then float back against the headrest, where she released one of those world-weary sighs like the woman in a book Eddie had read about this rich guy who loves this woman so much that he takes a hit-and-run rap for her.

"We just talked," Eddie said.

"Then she walked home."

Eddie saw the doubt in the detective's eyes. He didn't believe that Sheila had walked home. He believed that she'd been driven to some deserted section of Nickerson State Park and that Eddie had strangled her. Because it was in his blood, this murderousness.

"Tell me the very last thing you saw of Sheila, Eddie."

He saw her pull herself out into the faintly pinkish air. A breeze riffled her long dark hair. She drew back an errant strand, turned, and headed toward Breakwater Road. When she reached it, she looked back and smiled.

Eddie told the detective what he'd seen, leaving out the errant strand of dark brown hair.

"Did you see anybody following her?" the detective asked.

"No."

"Anything suspicious at all?"

"There was a van," Eddie said, then described it, dark green and dusty. It was parked on Breakwater, he told the detective, and sat low, as if weighted in the back.

"And Sheila, she was walking down Breakwater toward this van?"

"Yes," Eddie said, and saw her closing in behind it, then imagined a pair of eyes watching her in the van's cloudy rearview mirror, dark and sunken, his father's eyes.

"What's the matter, Eddie? You look a little shook up."

"I just hope she's all right, that's all."

"I'm sure you do," the detective said.

Eddie saw that the detective didn't believe a word of what he'd just told him. Weren't all missing girls snatched into vans? Wasn't that what the Coed Killer had done?

"How long have you known Sheila?"

"Three years."

"How would you describe your relationship?"

"We're friends."

"Just friends?"

Eddie saw that the detective's suspicion was full-blown now. There was no dusty green van. There was only Eddie and Sheila, and Eddie wanted her, but she didn't want him, and so they'd argued, and he'd . . .

"So there was nothing . . . romantic between you two?" the detective asked.

"No."

"Okay, after Sheila left, where did you go?"

"Home."

"So she went one way, and you went the other, right?"

"Yes."

He saw Sheila turn back and wave to him just before she wheeled left and headed down Breakwater. She had always been nice to him, always trusted him, even invited him to her house once. He'd said no to that, afraid of seeing that look in her parents' eyes as they opened the door and saw not just Eddie but the Old Man, too, standing there beside him.

"When you got home, was anybody there?"

"No."

No witnesses, then. Eddie saw that this was very important. No one to tell the detective that he'd come home and spent the rest of the afternoon reading this book about a rich kid who dreams of catching little girls in fields of rye. Not to hurt them, though. Only to save them from tumbling over a cliff.

"When did your mother get home?"

"Around seven."

He saw his mother hunched over the table in the kitchen, smoking a cigarette, still half-believing that it really didn't prove anything, the stains and hair, the skin beneath her husband's nails, the rope that matched, his teeth marks on their broken necks.

"So you were alone in the house from five until seven?"

"Yes."

And so, as Eddie saw, there'd been plenty of time for him to strangle Sheila Longstreet, find a place in Nickerson Park, and dig a nice deep hole.

"It's strange that Sheila would just disappear like that," the detective said. "Just half a mile from her house. With nobody else seeing her between the time you say she left you at the general store and now. So, tell me, Eddie, did she mention any problems she was having?"

They all had problems, Eddie knew, all the kids at school. He saw them sitting listlessly in class, getting high four times a day, with nothing to point the way, exert a force, give true direction. He saw Sheila in the car, her wide, searching eyes. What do you want, Sheila? To be left alone. They all said that, but Eddie saw that the last thing Sheila or any of them really wanted was to be left alone. What she wanted was an eye at her back, a hand on her shoulder, a world that didn't come at her like a meteor shower, time to think.

"Do you believe she ran away?" the detective asked.

Eddie saw that the detective's question wasn't really about Sheila. It was about him, Eddie Panacci. The detective was probing his mind, looking for a bead of sweat on the upper lip, a subtle shift of weight, listening for that sound Eddie had read about in a short story, the muffled thump of a telltale heart.

"We hear that Sheila's just about your only friend, Eddie," the detective said. "That you're sort of a loner, I mean."

Loner, Eddie saw, was the darkest of words. His father had been a loner. They all were, the guys in the dusty green vans.

"Okay, Eddie, let me ask you something else."

Eddie half-expected the detective to ask him straight out: How does it feel to be the Coed Killer's son? That was the question he saw in every mind, his teachers, kids at school. It hung there, like a noose.

"Some people had the idea that you were in love with Sheila," the detective said. "Any truth to that?"

Eddie wasn't sure. Maybe he'd felt about Sheila in a way he'd read about in a book about this old man who fights so hard to bring in this big fish that at last he comes to love it. She was restless wind and churning sea, and he saw that more than anything she wanted an end to this ceaseless agitation. A place in the harbor, that was what she wanted, a place in the harbor where the waters grew still and the moon was quiet, and beneath its calming gaze you became a gently lapping tide. And he wanted to help her find this peace, and he saw that this was love.

"No, I'm not in love with her," Eddie answered, knowing that this was not a lie, only a truth too complicated to explain.

The detective brought his face very near. "Eddie, tell me the truth, now. Do you have any idea where Sheila Longstreet is?"

Eddie saw that the detective was giving him a chance to come clean, to tell him the terrible truth that Sheila was in the basement or the pond, down a well, under a pile of bricks, rolled up in a carpet at the dump.

"No," he said. "I don't."

The detective drew back, and Eddie saw how frustrated he was, how he knew what Eddie had done but couldn't prove it, could only hope that Eddie would go home and do to himself what a fellow inmate had done to his father: take a shard of glass from a shattered mirror and plunge it into his neck.

"Are you sure, Eddie?"

"Yes."

"So you have nothing more you want to tell me, is that right?"

"I don't know anything else."

The detective drew a handkerchief from his back pocket and swabbed his face and the back of his neck. "Okay, you can go," he said wearily. "But don't leave the Cape."

On the way out of the parking lot, Eddie saw two kids from school as they were escorted into the police station. It was Terry Floyd and Donna Leone, both juniors. They weren't friends of Sheila's, and so he knew that their trouble was different from his, but they were in trouble all the same. He saw it in the careless sling of their arms, the indifferent slump of their shoulders, the way their heads hung heavy in the darkening air, so young, yet already oddly convinced that life had passed them by. He knew the feelings that pressed them down, their sense of being invisible to all eyes save those that watched them warily, or worriedly, or with a vague contempt.

At sixteen, they already saw themselves as losers, and so regarded life itself as lost, with nothing in it worth doing, nothing to reach for or attain. He watched Donna's hand crawl up the back of Terry's jacket, tug jokingly at his hair, then drop away when Terry made no response, and saw that if nothing changed, she would drop away from husbands, jobs, relations, drop away from struggle and achievement, the simple appreciation that all of life requires, drop away from everything with the same desultory gesture. The only energy she would ever have, he saw, was the slight amount it took to drop away, hopelessly and disdainfully, from anything in life that demanded more.

He got into his car and drove out of the lot, turning left on 6A, moving through the chill autumn air, past the old town hall and the library, until he reached the general store, where he decided to drop by the Longstreet house to tell Sheila's parents, for what it was worth, that he had not done their daughter any harm. He knew they wouldn't believe him, but he wanted to do it anyway, cry out, at least this once, that only in the most mysterious and impossible of ways was he the Coed Killer's son.

And so he turned eastward, toward the bay, following Breakwater for half a mile before the yellow beams of his headlights caught Sheila's red sweater and white skirt as she strolled unhurriedly along the side of the road.

She turned as he brought his car to a stop beside her, smiled when she saw him behind the wheel, and climbed in.

"Where have you been?" he asked.

"The woods behind the cemetery."

He saw the leaves that still clung to her sweater, the greenish smudge on her skirt. "You spent the night there?"

"I didn't want to go home."

"Everyone is looking for you. You should have told me you weren't going home."

"It just came over me, Eddie," Sheila said. "I got all the way to my house, all the way to the door, but then I saw my mom, my dad, you know, in the kitchen, and there were these, like, kitchen smells."

"They were making your dinner, Sheila," Eddie said. "What's wrong with that?"

She shrugged. "Anyway, I just couldn't . . ." That smile again. "You know what I mean, right?"

"I'll take you home."

"Okay."

He drove down the street and turned into the driveway of Sheila's house. She got out quickly. "Thanks, Eddie," she said brightly. "See you in school tomorrow."

"Yeah."

She headed for the door, drawing the red sweater from her shoulders, dragging it behind her across the carefully tended lawn. She was halfway to the house when her father rushed out and pulled his missing daughter into his arms. Her mother was at the door by then, her hand at her mouth, crying. A parent's love was never in the words, Eddie saw, never in the money or the things that lay in piles in bedrooms and garages. It was in their desperate hope that you were okay.

His mother was still at work when he reached home. He made himself a sandwich, washed it down with soda, then walked onto the porch and stared up at the sky. He remembered the question the detective had not asked: How does it feel to be the Coed Killer's son? Eddie saw that he had an answer now.

Blessed.

Blessed because he saw things through the prism of the Old Man's crime: the two young women, not much older than himself, whose lives his father had cut short, and who, had they been given another chance to live, would no doubt have treasured the most ordinary things, held dearly to what was truly dear, found all the meaning of life they needed in the simple living of it.

He was the Coed Killer's son, and because of that, he saw nothing meager in life's feast of days, nothing empty in its promise of a wife, kids, a decent job, and so did not look forward to the coming years in a mood of sullen ire. He thought of Sheila, Terry, Donna, other kids at school, and hoped that they might finally come to see what he so clearly saw. That if they raised a family, worked, laughed a little, found some form of enduring love, gained what could be gained from the journey, then it would be enough.

No, Eddie saw, it would be . . . so much.

WHAT SHE OFFERED

"Sounds like a dangerous woman," my friend said. He'd not been with me in the bar the night before, not seen her leave or me follow after her.

I took a sip of vodka and glanced toward the window. Outside, the afternoon light was no doubt as it had always been, but it didn't look the same to me anymore. "I guess she was," I told him.

"So what happened?" my friend asked.

This: I was in the bar. It was two in the morning. The people around me were like tapes from *Mission: Impossible*, only without the mission, just that self-destruct warning. You could almost hear it playing in their heads, stark and unyielding as the Chinese proverb: *If you continue down the road you're on, you will get to where you're headed.*

Where were they headed? As I saw it, mostly toward more of the same. They would finish this drink, this night, this week . . . and so on. At some point, they would die like animals after a long, exhausting haul, numb with weariness as they finally slumped beneath the burden. Worse still, according to me, this bar was the world, its few dully buzzing flies no more than stand-ins for the rest of us.

I had written about "us" in novel after novel. My tone was always bleak. In my books, there were no happy endings. People were lost and helpless, even the smart ones . . . especially the smart ones. Everything was in vain and everything was fleeting. The strongest emotions quickly waned. A few things mattered, but only because we made them matter by insisting that they should. If we needed evidence of this, we made it up. As far as I could tell, there were basically three kinds of people, the ones who deceived others, the ones who deceived themselves, and the ones who understood that the people in the first two categories were the only ones they were ever likely to meet. I put myself firmly in the third category, of course, the only member of my club, the one guy who understood that to see things in full light was the greatest darkness one could know.

And so I walked the streets and haunted the bars and was, according to me, the only man on earth who had nothing to learn.

Then, suddenly, she walked through the door.

To black, she offered one concession. A string of small white pearls. Everything else, the hat, the dress, the stockings, the shoes, the little purse . . . everything else was black. And so, what she offered at that first glimpse was just the old B-movie stereotype of the dangerous woman, the broad-billed hat that discreetly covers one eye, high heels tapping on rain-slicked streets, foreign currency in the small black purse. She offered the spy, the murderess, the lure of a secret past, and, of course, that little hint of erotic peril.

She knows the way men think, I said to myself as she walked to the end of the bar and took her seat. She knows the way they think . . . and she's using it.

"So you thought she was what?" my friend asked.

I shrugged. "Inconsequential."

And so I watched without interest as the melo-dramatic touches accumulated. She lit a cigarette and smoked it pensively, her eyes opening and closing languidly, with the sort of world-weariness one sees in the heroines of old black-and-white movies.

Yes, that's it, I told myself. She is *noir* in the worst possible sense, thin as strips of film and just as transparent at the edges. I looked at my watch. Time to go, I thought, time to go to my apartment and stretch out on the bed and wallow in my dark superiority, congratulate myself that once again I had not been fooled by the things that fool other men.

But it was only two in the morning, early for me, so I lingered in the bar, and wondered, though only vaguely, with no more than passing interest, if she had anything else to offer beyond this show of being "dangerous."

"Then what?" my friend asked.

Then she reached in her purse, drew out a small black pad, flipped it open, wrote something, and passed it down the bar to me.

The paper was folded, of course. I unfolded it and read what she'd written: *I know what you know about life.*

It was exactly the kind of nonsense I'd expected, so I briskly scrawled a reply on the back of the paper and sent it down the bar to her.

She opened it and read what I'd written: *No, you don't. And you never will.* Then, without so much as looking up, she wrote a lightning-fast response and sent it hurtling back up the bar, quickly gathering her things and heading for the door as it went from hand to hand, so that she'd already left the place by the time it reached me.

I opened the note and read her reply: C+.

My anger spiked. C+? How dare she! I whirled around on the stool and rushed out of the bar, where I found her leaning casually against the little wrought-iron fence that surrounded it.

I waved the note in front of her. "What's this supposed to mean?" I demanded.

She smiled and offered me a cigarette. "I've read your books. They're really dreadful."

I don't smoke, but I took the cigarette anyway. "So, you're a critic?"

She gave no notice to what I'd just said. "The writing is beautiful," she said as she lit my cigarette with a red plastic lighter. "But the idea is really bad."

"Which idea is that?"

"You only have one," she said with total confidence. "That everything ends badly, no matter what we do." Her face tightened. "So, here's the deal. When I wrote, *I know what you know about life*, that wasn't exactly true. I know more."

I took a long drag on the cigarette. "So," I asked lightly. "Is this a date?"

She shook her head, and suddenly her eyes grew dark and somber. "No," she said, "this is a love affair."

I started to speak, but she lifted her hand and stopped me.

"I could do it with you, you know," she whispered, her voice now very grave. "Because you know almost as much as I do, and I want to do it with someone who knows that much."

From the look in her eyes I knew exactly what she wanted to "do" with me. "We'd need a gun," I told her with a dismissive grin.

She shook her head. "I'd never use a gun. It would be pills." She let her cigarette drop from her fingers. "And we'd need to be in bed together," she added matter-of-factly. "Naked and in each other's arms."

"Why is that?"

Her smile was soft as light. "To show the world that you were wrong." The smile widened, almost playfully. "That something can end well."

"Suicide?" I asked. "You call that ending well?"

She laughed and tossed her hair slightly. "It's the only way to end well," she said.

And I thought, *she's nuts*, but for the first time in years, I wanted to hear more.

—◁◦▷—

"A suicide pact," my friend whispered.

"That's what she offered, yes," I told him. "But not right away. She said that there was something I needed to do first."

"What?"

"Fall in love with her," I answered quietly.

"And she knew you would?" my friend asked. "Fall in love with her, I mean?"

"Yes, she did," I told him.

But she also knew that the usual process was fraught with trials, a road scattered with pits and snares. So she'd decided to forgo courtship, the tedious business of exchanging mounds of trivial biographical information. Physical intimacy would come first, she said. It was the gate through which we would enter each other.

"So, we should go to my place now," she concluded, after offering her brief explanation of all this. "We need to fuck."

"Fuck?" I laughed. "You're not exactly the romantic type, are you?"

"You can undress me if you want to," she said. "Or, if not, I'll do it myself."

"Maybe you should do it," I said jokingly. "That way I won't dislocate your shoulder."

She laughed. "I get suspicious if a man does it really well. It makes me think that he's a bit too familiar with all those female clasps and snaps and zippers. It makes me wonder if perhaps he's . . . worn it all himself."

"Jesus," I moaned. "You actually think about things like that?"

Her gaze and tone became deadly serious. "I can't handle every need," she said.

There was a question in her eyes, and I knew what the question was. She wanted to know if I had any secret cravings or odd sexual quirks, any "needs" she could not "handle."

"I'm strictly double-vanilla," I assured her. "No odd flavors."

She appeared slightly relieved. "My name is Veronica," she said.

"I was afraid you weren't going to tell me," I said. "That it was going to be one of those things where I never know who you are and vice versa. You know, ships that pass in the night."

"How banal that would be," she said.

"Yes, it would."

"Besides," she added, "I already knew who you were."

"Yes, of course."

"My apartment is just down the block," she said, then offered to take me there.

———◇———

As it turned out, her place was a bit farther than just down the block, but it didn't matter. It was after two in the morning and the streets were pretty much deserted. Even in New York, certain streets, especially certain Greenwich Village streets, are never all that busy, and once people have gone to and from work, they become little more than country lanes. That night the trees that lined Jane Street swayed gently in the cool autumn air, and I let myself accept what I thought she'd offered, which, for all the "dangerous" talk, would probably be no more than a brief erotic episode, maybe breakfast in the morning, a little light conversation over coffee and scones. Then she would go her way and I would go mine because one of us would want it that way and the other wouldn't care enough to argue the point.

"The vodka's in the freezer," she said as she opened the door to her apartment, stepped inside and switched on the light.

I walked into the kitchen while Veronica headed down a nearby corridor. The refrigerator was at the far end of the room, its freezer door festooned with pictures of Veronica and a short, bald little man who looked to be in his late forties.

"That's Douglas," Veronica called from somewhere down the hall. "My husband."

I felt a pinch of apprehension.

"He's away," she added.

The apprehension fled.

"I should hope so," I said as I opened the freezer door.

Veronica's husband faced me again when I closed it, the ice-encrusted vodka bottle now securely in my right hand. Now I noticed that Douglas was somewhat portly, deep lines around his eyes, graying at the temples. Okay, I thought, maybe mid-fifties. And yet, for all that, he had a boyish face. In the pictures, Veronica towered over him, his bald head barely reaching her broad shoulders. She was in every photograph, his arm always wrapped affectionately around her waist. And in every photograph Douglas was smiling with such unencumbered joy that I knew that all his happiness came from her, from being with her, being her husband, that when he was with her he felt tall and dark and handsome, witty and smart and perhaps even a bit elegant. That was what she offered him, I supposed, the illusion that he deserved her.

"He was a bartender when I met him," she said as she swept into the kitchen. "Now he sells software." She lifted an impossibly long and graceful right arm to the cabinet at her side, opened its plain wooden doors and retrieved two decidedly ordinary glasses, which she placed squarely on the plain Formica counter before turning to face me. "From the beginning, I was always completely comfortable with Douglas," she said.

She could not have said it more clearly. Douglas was the man she had chosen to marry because he possessed whatever characteristics she required to feel absolutely at home when she was at home, utterly herself when she was with him. If there had been some great love in her life, she had chosen Douglas over him because with Douglas she could live without change or alteration, without applying makeup to her soul. Because of that, I suddenly found myself feeling vaguely envious of this squat little man, of the peace he gave her, the way she could no doubt rest in the crook of his arm, breathing slowly, falling asleep.

"He seems . . . nice," I said.

Veronica gave no indication that she'd heard me. "You take it straight," she said, referring to the way I took my drink, which was clearly something she'd noticed in the bar.

I nodded.

"Me, too."

She poured our drinks and directed me into the living room. The curtains were drawn tightly together and looked a bit dusty. The furniture had been chosen for comfort rather than style. There were a few potted plants, most of them brown at the edges. You could almost hear them begging for water. No dogs. No cats. No goldfish or hamsters or snakes or white mice. When Douglas was away, it appeared, Veronica lived alone.

Except for books, but they were everywhere. They filled shelf after towering shelf, or lay stacked to the point of toppling along the room's four walls. The authors ran the gamut, from the oldest classics to the most recent bestsellers. Stendahl and Dostoyevsky rested shoulder to shoulder with Anne Rice and Michael Crichton. A few of my own stark titles were lined up between Robert Stone and Patrick O'Brian. There was no history or social science in her collection, and no poetry. It was all fiction, as Veronica herself seemed to be, a character she'd made up and was determined to play to the end. What she offered, I believed at that moment, was a well-rounded performance of a New York eccentric.

She touched her glass to mine, her eyes very still. "To what we're going to do," she said.

"Are we still talking about committing suicide together?" I scoffed as I lowered my glass without drinking. "What is this, Veronica? Some kind of *Sweet November* rewrite?"

"I don't know what you mean," she said.

"You know, that stupid movie where the dying girl takes this guy and lives with him for a month and—"

"I would never live with you," Veronica interrupted.

"That's not my point."

"And I'm not dying," Veronica added. She took a quick sip of vodka, placed her glass onto the small table beside the sofa, then, as if suddenly called by an invisible voice, offered her hand to me. "Time for bed," she said.

———◇———

"Just like that?" my friend asked.

"Just like that."

He looked at me warily. "This is a fantasy, right?" he asked. "This is something you made up."

"What happened next no one could make up."

"And what was that?"

She led me to the bedroom. We undressed silently. She crawled beneath the single sheet and patted the mattress. "This side is yours."

"Until Douglas gets back," I said as I drew in beside her.

"Douglas isn't coming back," she said, then leaned over and kissed me very softly.

"Why not?"

"Because he's dead," she answered lightly. "He's been dead for over three years."

And thus I learned of her husband's slow decline, the cancer that began in his intestines and migrated to his liver and pancreas. It had taken six months, and each day Veronica had attended him. She would look in on him on her way to work every morning, then return to him at night, stay at his bedside until she was sure he would not awaken, then, at last, return here, to this very bed, to sleep for an hour or two, three at the most, before beginning the routine again.

"Six months," I said. "That's a long time."

"A dying person is a lot of work," she said.

"Yes, I know," I told her. "I was with my father when he died. I was exhausted by the time he finally went."

"Oh, I don't mean that," she said. "The physical part. The lack of sleep. That wasn't the hardest part when it came to Douglas."

"What was?"

"Making him believe I loved him."

"You didn't?"

"No," she said, then kissed me again, a kiss that lingered a bit longer than the first, and gave me time to remember that just a few minutes before she'd told me that Douglas was currently selling software.

"Software," I said, drawing my lips from hers. "You said he sold software now."

She nodded. "Yes, he does."

"To other dead people?" I lifted myself up and propped my head in my hand. "I can't wait for an explanation."

"There is no explanation," she said. "Douglas always wanted to sell software. So, instead of saying that he's in the ground or in heaven, I just say he's selling software."

"So you give death a cute name," I said. "And that way you don't have to face it."

"I say he's selling software because I don't want the conversation that would follow if I told you he was dead," Veronica said sharply. "I hate consolation."

"Then why did you tell me at all?"

"Because you need to know that I'm like you," she answered. "Alone. That no one will mourn."

"So we're back to suicide again," I said. "Do you always circle back to death?"

She smiled. "Do you know what La Rochefoucauld said about death?"

"It's not on the tip of my tongue, no."

"He said that it was like the sun. You couldn't look at it for very long without going blind." She shrugged. "But I think that if you look at it all the time, measure it against living, then you can choose."

I drew her into my arms. "You're a bit quirky, Veronica," I said playfully.

She shook her head, her voice self-assured. "No," she insisted. "I'm the sanest person you've ever met."

———◦———

"And she was," I told my friend.

"What do you mean?"

"I mean she offered more than anyone I'd ever known."

"What did she offer?"

That night she offered the cool, sweet luxury of her flesh, a kiss that so brimmed with feeling I thought her lips would give off sparks.

We made love for a time then, suddenly, she stopped and pulled away. "Time to chat," she said, then walked to the kitchen and returned with another two glasses of vodka.

"Time to chat?" I asked, still disconcerted with how abruptly she'd drawn away from me.

"I don't have all night," she said as she offered me the glass.

I took the drink from her hand. "So we're not going to toast the dawn together?"

She sat on the bed, cross-legged and naked, her body sleek and smooth in the blue light. "You're glib," she said as she clinked her glass to mine. "So am I." She leaned forward slightly, her eyes glowing in the dark. "Here is the deal," she added. "If you're glib, you finally get to the end of what you can say. There are no words left for anything important. Just sleek words. Clever. Glib. That's when you know you've gone as far as you can go, that you have nothing left to offer but smooth talk."

"That's rather harsh, don't you think?" I took a sip of vodka. "And besides, what's the alternative to talking?"

"Silence," Veronica answered.

I laughed. "Veronica, you are hardly silent."

"Most of the time, I am," she said.

"And what does this silence conceal?"

"Anger," she answered without the slightest hesitation. "Fury."

Her face grew taut, and I thought the rage I suddenly glimpsed within her would set her hair ablaze.

"Of course you can get to silence in other ways," she said. She took a quick, brutal drink from her glass. "Douglas got there, but not by being glib."

"How then?"

"By suffering."

I looked for her lip to tremble, but it didn't. I looked for moisture in her eyes, but they were dry and still.

"By being terrified," she added. She glanced toward the window, let her gaze linger there for a moment, then returned to me. "The last week he didn't say a word," she said. "That's when I knew it was time."

"Time for what?"

"Time for Douglas to get a new job."

I felt my heart stop dead. "In . . . software?" I asked.

She lit a candle, placed it on the narrow shelf above us, then yanked open the top drawer of the small table that sat beside her bed, retrieved a plastic pill case and shook it so that I could hear the pills rattling dryly inside it.

"I'd planned to give him these," she said, "but there wasn't time."

"What do you mean, there wasn't time?"

"I saw it in his face," she answered. "He was living like someone already in the ground. Someone buried and waiting for the air to give out. That kind of suffering, terror. I knew that one additional minute would be too long."

She placed the pills on the table, then grabbed the pillow upon which her head had rested, fluffed it gently, pressed it down upon my face, then lifted it again in a way that made me feel strangely returned to life. "It was all I had left to offer him," she said quietly, then took a long, slow pull on the vodka. "We have so little to offer."

And I thought with sudden, devastating clarity, *Her darkness is real; mine is just a pose.*

———◇———

"What did you do?" my friend asked.

"I touched her face."

"And what did she do?"

She pulled my hand away almost violently. "This isn't about me," she said.

"Right now, everything is about you," I told her.

She grimaced. "Bullshit."

"I mean it."

"Which only makes it worse," she said sourly. Her eyes rolled upward, then came down again, dark and steely, like the twin barrels of a shotgun. "This is about you," she said crisply. "And I won't be cheated of it."

I shrugged. "All life is a cheat, Veronica."

Her eyes tensed. "That isn't true and you know it," she said, her voice almost a hiss. "And because of that you are a liar, and all your books are lies." Her voice was so firm, so hard and unrelenting, I felt it like a wind. "Here's the deal," she said. "If you really felt the way you write, you'd kill yourself. If all that feeling was really in you, down deep in you, you wouldn't be able to live a single day." She dared me to contradict her, and when I didn't, she said, "You see everything but yourself. And here's what you don't see about yourself, Jack. You don't see that you're happy."

"Happy?" I asked.

"You are happy," Veronica insisted. "You won't admit it, but you are. And you should be."

Then she offered the elements of my happiness, the sheer good fortune I had enjoyed, health, adequate money, work I loved, little dollops of achievement.

"Compared to you, Douglas had nothing," she said.

"He had you," I said cautiously.

Her face soured again. "If you make it about me," she warned, "you'll have to leave."

She was serious, and I knew it. So I said, "What do you want from me, Veronica?"

Without hesitation she said, "I want you to stay."

"Stay?"

"While I take the pills."

I remembered the line she'd said just outside the bar only a few hours before, *I could do it with you, you know.*

I had taken this to mean that we would do it together, but now I knew that she had never included me. There was no pact. There was only Veronica.

"Will you do it?" she asked somberly.

"When?" I asked quietly.

She took the pills and poured them into her hand. "Now," she said.

"No," I blurted, and started to rise.

She pressed me down hard, her gaze relentlessly determined, so that I knew that she would do what she intended, that there was no way to stop her.

"I want out of this noise," she said, pressing her one empty hand to her right ear. "Everything is so loud."

In the fierceness of those words I glimpsed the full measure of her torment, all she no longer wished to hear, the clanging daily vanities and thudding repetitions, the catcalls of the inferior, the trumpeting mediocrities, all of which lifted to a soul-searing roar the unbearable clatter of the wheel. She wanted an end to all of that, a silence she would not be denied.

"Will you stay?" she asked quietly.

I knew that any argument would strike her as just more noise she could not bear. It would clang like cymbals, only add to the mindless cacophony she was so desperate to escape.

And so I said, "All right."

With no further word, she swallowed the pills two at a time, washing them down with quick sips of vodka.

"I don't know what to say to you, Veronica," I told her when she took the last of them and put down the glass.

She curled under my arm. "Say what I said to Douglas," she told me. "In the end it's all anyone can offer."

"What did you say to him?" I asked softly.

"I'm here."

I drew my arm tightly around her. "I'm here," I said.

She snuggled in more closely. "Yes."

—◦—

"And so you stayed?" my friend asked.

I nodded.

"And she . . ."

"In about an hour," I told him. "Then I dressed and walked the streets until I finally came here."

"So right now she's . . ."

"Gone," I said quickly, and suddenly imagined her sitting in the park across from the bar, still and silent.

"You couldn't stop her?"

"With what?" I asked. "I had nothing to offer." I glanced out the front window of the bar. "And besides," I added, "for a truly dangerous woman, a man is never the answer. That's what makes her dangerous. At least, to us."

My friend looked at me oddly. "So what are you going to do now?" he asked.

At the far end of the park a young couple was screaming at each other, the woman's fist in the air, the man shaking his head in violent confusion. I could imagine Veronica turning from them, walking silently away.

"I'm going to keep quiet," I answered. "For a very long time."

Then I got to my feet and walked out into the whirling city. The usual dissonance engulfed me, all the chaos and disarray, but I felt no need to add my own inchoate discord to the rest.

It was a strangely sweet feeling, I realized as I turned and headed home, embracing silence.

From deep within her enveloping calm, Veronica offered me her final words.

I know.